Copyright © 20

All rights reserved

The characters and events portrayed in this book are fictitious. Any similarity to real persons, living or dead, is coincidental and not intended by the author.

No part of this book may be reproduced, or stored in a retrieval system, or transmitted in any form or by any means, electronic, mechanical, photocopying, recording, or otherwise, without express written permission of the publisher.

ISBN-13: 9798692948489
ISBN-10: 1477123456

Cover design by: Mike Beckom
Library of Congress Control Number: 2018675309
Printed in the United Kingdom

For Briony

THE MONSTER AT THE MOONLIGHT HOTEL

By Joshua James Potts

DAY ZERO

PROLOGUE

When I heard that the year 7 pupils would be going on a trip to Cornwall, I packed as many books as I could. Maybe if I could stay in the world of zombies and vampires, I wouldn't notice my stupid classmates or unfair teachers. The one I was reading now was called *Rollercoaster of the Dead*. It was about a theme park where the rides were alive. It was pretty cool, but I dropped it when a fist whacked me on the back of the head.

"Pay attention, idiot." The boy behind me pointed to Mr Morris, who was reading the register.

"Jack Williams. Are you here, Jack Williams?" he asked, looking right at me.

"Present, sir," I said, and pulled my book back over to me with my foot. The cover was all dusty and dirty where it had dragged on the floor of the bus. There was a mark like the bottom of my shoe on the other side. I wiped it with my sleeve.

The road was really thin and there were old-fashioned houses on each side made of old stone and red roofs. I worried about how fast the bus was going on such a small road, especially since the sign said we were coming up to a bridge.

"What's so funny about the bridge?" I asked.

"What's that, boy?" said Mr Morris

"That sign said, "Laughter Bridge coming up". What's so funny about the bridge? Did they used to tell jokes there or something?"

I thought this was going to be an interesting bit of history but instead, Mr Morris muttered "Don't say stupid things," and turned away.

"Idiot," the boy behind me said again. "That sign didn't say Laughter Bridge. It said Slaughter Bridge. You know, like killing people!" He mimed stabbing the girl next to him, who was peeing herself laughing at my mistake.

"You're the idiots. Both of you," I said and looked out of the window again. It turned out he was right. "Slaughter Bridge." The bridge looked really old. I wondered if it was built by the Romans. I liked the Romans. We did them in history.

I thought we must be nearly there because everything seemed so green and quiet. It didn't look anything like where I grew up. If you don't know Cornwall, it's right at the bottom-left of England, by the sea. There are loads of cool myths about pirates and mysterious beasts. Despite the stupid people I was going with, I was really excited to go to Cornwall for one big reason. I didn't remember ever being there, but I knew that it was where my birth parents were from. I'd asked so many questions but "They're from Cornwall" was all I could get out of my auntie and uncle who raised me. I knew it was a long shot, but I wondered if maybe – just, maybe – I could find my parents on this trip.

There was another reason I wanted to go, and that reason was Ruby Davies. Ruby was the smartest kid in our school, and she had a really pretty smile. I loved to see her laugh, because when she did, she grinned really wide and got dimples in her cheeks. Actually no, she didn't. She got *one* dimple, right in the corner of her left cheek. Ruby and I had been friends since primary school. Sadly, we weren't in any of the same classes anymore because she was so much smarter than I was. I was really excited to spend some time with her on this trip.

Sarah – my auntie – was really excited for me to go too. She and Paul were going away that week, and "Can't do with looking after you two at the same time." That was why Grace was going as well. Grace was their daughter – my cousin. She was the blonde girl who was sat behind me on the bus cuddling up to the kid who punched me in the back of the head. Not that she cared about Cornwall. She just wanted to be with her boyfriend, Thomas, when their parents weren't around to see what they were getting up to. Disgusting.

I brought in my completed application the morning

after the holiday was announced. I was so excited. I wanted to get on the bus right that minute. But Mr Morris wasn't in his classroom. *That makes sense,* I had thought, *I did come in really early.* I left my application on his desk and was about to leave when I noticed a list of names. Not printed out, just handwritten. It was the name of each of the kids who'd been picked to go on the trip. Grace was there, and Thomas and Ruby. But only my name was circled in thick, red ink.

CHAPTER 1
<u>Don't Talk to Strangers</u>

The bus stopped at a service station so that we could get some lunch. As soon as the doors opened, we all ran. We could hear Mr Morris shouting at us that we shouldn't get lost but we didn't listen. Everyone was loose with their own money and no parents to tell them how to spend it. I used some of my money to buy Ruby and me a meal from McDonald's. She told me that I didn't need to pay for hers, but I insisted.

"Tintagel is actually where I was born," I said, as I put my backpack on the seat next to me and sat down. "I don't remember it though. My auntie told me I was actually born in the sea."

"Wow, I bet you're a great swimmer."

"Are you kidding? I'm useless!"

"Oh, Jack. It's really easy. I'll teach you how, if you want."

"Really?"

"Sure. Everyone should know how to swim. You

know, for safety and that."

I'd heard that enough times. I'd been told how important it was to swim all my life. The truth is, I was terrified of the water and had probably never been near the sea since I was a baby.

But all I said was, "That sounds really good, thanks."

"Don't worry about it. I've been swimming my whole life. My grandma takes me all the time. We love it."

I knew that Ruby lived with her grandmother, but I didn't know why. Whenever anyone mentioned her parents, she got really upset, so I'd never asked. But she seemed happy. She loved her grandma.

"I'm really excited to see Tintagel Castle," Ruby continued.

"Oh yeah. I thought you'd like that. You're so good at history. You'll love it. I'll show you around. I've read loads about it."

Our conversation was interrupted by a loud outburst from behind us. "Oh, Thomas! It's beautiful!" Apparently, Thomas had won Grace a bracelet in the arcades.

Mr Morris went around telling everyone to make sure they went to the toilet before they got back on the bus. Ruby and I finished our food, put our rubbish in the bin and split off to go to the toilets. The queue was enormous.

Some boys I recognised but didn't really know stood behind me. The man in front of me stank and looked crazy. He had a huge dirty beard, so it was impossible to work out how big his face actually was. He had thick square glasses and tiny little black eyes underneath.

"Pretty girl, that one," he said. "Is that your girlfriend?" The boys behind me sniggered.

"No. Just some girl. A friend."

He chuckled. "Well, boy. You've got a pretty friend."

The boys laughed again. I turned to talk to them, and to put my back to this crazy guy.

"What are you guys talking about?" I asked.

"We were just saying what we're going to do when we get to the hotel."

"Oh yeah?"

"Johnny brought his PlayStation. If there's a TV, we'll link it up and play all night. We're not going to sleep all week!"

"Wait. What do you mean *if*? You don't think there'll be a TV?" I asked.

"You haven't seen the pictures? The hotel is really old. We'll be lucky if it has wi-fi."

"Don't be stupid," I said. "The school wouldn't take us somewhere without wi-fi. That's against our human rights or something."

"Kids these days," muttered the smelly guy. We ignored him.

"Where did you see the pictures?"

"Googled it. It hasn't even got a website though." One of the kids held up his phone. I could make out some old wooden building that looked like it was falling over. "Just some pictures that people have taken when they were complaining. Look here. DO NOT GO TO MOONLIGHT HOTEL. Our room had clearly not been cleaned. The food was inedible and the plug in the bath was clogged with long hair. By the end of the trip, my wife and I were arguing, and my son has stopped speaking entirely. DO NOT GO TO MOONLIGHT HOTEL."

When he said this, the smelly man stopped pretending he wasn't listening and just turned to face us.

"It can't be that bad," I said. "They always exaggerate on those things."

"Don't be stupid, Jack."

"What did you just say?" said that man.

"It was just some stupid review on Google, man. Chill."

"Are you going to the Moonlight Hotel?"

I shrugged. "School trip."

"No!" he screamed. "You cannot! You can't go there." He grabbed my shoulders.

"Get off!"

"Hey. Get off him, man!"

The kids ran. I tried to pull away.

"Listen, boy. You've got to come with me. I'll keep you safe. I'll take you somewhere where nobody will find you. But you cannot go to that hotel."

"Get off!"

"Excuse me, what on Earth do you think you're doing? Get off that boy."

It was Mr Morris. The man let go of my shoulders.

"Well? Do you have an explanation?"

I thought the man was going to punch Mr Morris. That would've been cool. Instead, he stood really close to his face and squinted.

"You cannot take these children to that hotel. What is wrong with you?"

"Where we are going and what we are doing there is none of your business, I think you'll find. Now, I suggest you get out of here before I tell the police that you were grabbing one of my students."

"How dare you," he countered. "You're one of *them*, aren't you?"

"Excuse me?" Mr Morris looked confused and then looked as though he noticed something about the man. "Have I met you before?"

The man instantly backed away. "No! Never mind. I'm going. You don't need to worry about me."

Mr Morris patted one of the boys on the back. A little too hard by the look on his face.

"You did the right thing, boys. Jack, why didn't you do anything? Why didn't you scream?"

"I wasn't going to scream!"

"Well, maybe if you had, I'd have been able to rescue you sooner. You should think a little more, Jack. Hurry up and go to the toilet, boys, and then come straight back to the bus."

With that, he walked outside.

I muttered a thanks and turned away. We joined the queue again but didn't speak after that. We waited our turns, went in and used the toilet in silence. I washed my hands and could see the boys leaving in the mirror. They were talking and laughing again but had clearly not wanted to stay with me.

Oh well, I thought as I walked back to the bus. *It's not like I need them anyway. I'll just spend the holiday with Ruby, and if she isn't interested, I always have my book.*

My book! I reached around and patted my back, as though I might have been wrong. I realised that I had left my bag at the table where we had eaten lunch.

I walked up to the window and looked in. There it was! Right where I'd been sitting.

"Come on, Jack. We're leaving!" shouted Mr Morris.

"Just a minute. I need to get my bag. Wait for me," I called back.

I ran back through the double doors, telling myself that I would just be a minute. In and out.

I pulled the chair out and my rucksack was on the seat where I had been sat. I unzipped it and stuck my hand in. I could feel several paperback books. I zipped the bag back up and threw it over my shoulder. I made to run straight back to the bus.

Except, as I tried to run, I felt two big, strong arms wrap around me and lift me straight up off the floor.

CHAPTER 2

<u>Snatched!</u>

I was lifted one foot, two feet, three feet off the floor. I kicked my legs underneath, but I couldn't reach.

"Stop wriggling," a voice growled in my ear. His beard scratched my neck and I could smell old coffee on his breath.

Through the windows, I could see the other kids getting onto the bus. Ruby was gazing around, and I wondered if she was searching for me. Finally, she gave up and climbed onto the bus as well. She walked past Mr Morris and climbed the stairs.

Mr Morris!

My attacker must have known what I was going to do because a big fatty hand squeezed over my mouth and the mysterious man growled into my ear, "You wouldn't even think of screaming if you knew what was good for you, little man. You're coming with me, you are."

I tried to scream No! But all that came out was a muffled "Nmmmmm."

I wriggled my body as quickly and violently as I could. He was stronger than me, but I was younger. I was able to bend my arm backwards and I slipped out of my backpack. I fell to the ground on my palms with a splat.

My hands felt sore. I got up and ran as fast as I could. I wanted to look behind me, but I worried that any moment I spent doing that would slow me down.

I wondered if he was following me, but when I got outside, Mr Morris spotted me and shouted, "Mr Williams, you have held our trip up for quite long enough now! If you're quite ready, would you get on this bus, so that we can get going?"

I was too tired to respond but I stepped onto the bus. I glanced over my shoulder and I could see the man waiting by the door of the service station. It was the man who'd been scaring us all in the queue for the toilets! He stood watching me for a moment through his thick glasses and then sat down to look through my backpack.

My backpack! He still had it!

I patted down my pockets. Oh no! Not only did he have my clothes and toothbrush, he had my phone! Now I had no way of contacting anyone back home. And worse still (the thought gave me chills), what if he started texting people and pretending to be me? I wanted to contact my auntie and warn her, but how could I? I didn't have my phone. And even if I used the teacher's, I didn't know her number.

I dragged my feet sadly as I walked down the bus to find a seat. I saw Grace and Thomas laughing at me. "What took you so long?" Thomas asked. I didn't say anything. I just kept walking. I picked *Rollercoaster of the Dead* up off one of the seats. Ruby cleared a space for me to sit with her.

"Where's your bag?" she asked.

"That guy took it," I said, and I looked out of the window for him.

At first, I couldn't see him. But then I did. His face jumped up at my window. He banged on the glass really hard with his fist.

"No!" he cried. "You can't go! Don't go to that hotel, Jack Williams!"

I wanted to ask him how he knew my name, but I didn't have chance as the bus left the service station and drove back onto the motorway.

"That was crazy," Ruby said. "Who was that man?"

"I don't know. Just some weird guy, I guess."

"Was there anything expensive in your bag?"

I thought about that. My phone was hardly expensive. It was my Paul's old one, an ancient thing that still had buttons on the front.

"Not really. I mean, all my clothes were in there. And my toothbrush and stuff."

"Eww," she said. "You're going to stink by the end of this trip, Jack." I blushed.

CHAPTER 3
<u>The Moonlight hotel</u>

"There it is folks. Put your electronic devices down and look at your home for the coming week."

Mr Morris slammed my book shut so that I'd pay attention. I thought that this was unfair, because my book wasn't an electronic device, and besides, I'd been getting to the really good bit. Christian, the hero of the story, had had his leg torn off by the zombies. Rather than admit defeat, he had fastened a flame thrower to the stump and was giving those zombies hell. I'd read the book a hundred times – the cover was falling off – and it was my favourite part of any book I'd ever read.

But I wouldn't get to read it on this trip. Instead, I was looking out of the coach window at-

"*That's* where we're going to stay?" Grace exclaimed.

Mr Morris either misread her open jaw or intentionally decided to ignore it. "Magnificent, isn't it?" he said. "The Moonlight Hotel has stood here for over two hundred years. Yet still, the old gal is hanging on."

"*Hanging on* is right," Ruby whispered.

"Barely," I replied. We both laughed.

The Moonlight Hotel was an old rickety building that was barely clinging to the dangerous looking bit of cliff that it was stuck on to. The cliff grew frighteningly thin as it stretched over the crashing waves of the Atlantic Ocean beneath and looked as though it was preparing to crumble away itself, never mind the shoddily thrown together stack of wood that sat on top of it.

"Look," said Ruby. "Do you see all the different colours of wood? That means they've had to replace bits that have broken."

"This can't be safe," Grace said.

"Of course, it's safe, children. Now, get your things. Who's excited?"

Mr Morris gave a little jump and punched the air enthusiastically. The other kids and I exchanged worried glances. Thomas, I noticed, was holding on to Grace's hand. I looked at Ruby's hand.

"Mr Williams, why are you not collecting your bag?"

"I haven't got my bag, sir. It was stolen."

"Well, that was very careless of you. I hope that you're going to be a little more conscientious on the rest of this trip."

"I'll try not to lose it *again*."

"That's the spirit. Now, off the bus. All of you."

I threw my coat on and got off the bus.

"Come on," I heard Mr Morris shouting. "That means all of you. You haven't all lost your bags. Hurry up."

I jumped back in horror and knocked the next kid over.

"Oi. What the hell do you think you're doing?"

"Witch!" was all I could say. I held my hand out and pointed at the hunched-up figure stood by the door of the hotel.

She was even more crooked than the hotel. She was bent over a wooden stick and had an enormous lump on her back. She wore a black dress and her long knots of black hair had probably never seen shampoo. She looked right at me. Not just in my general direction but right into my eyes. I scrambled to my feet and she moved her stick forwards. She was coming right towards me. I couldn't believe that a woman who looked like that could walk as fast as she could. Before I knew it, she was directly in front of me.

The ground was wet and covered in some sort of slimy mud. As I tried to run, my feet couldn't grip the floor and I kept falling. I screamed.

"Williams! What the hell are you doing?"

I tried to steady myself as Mr Morris pulled me up by my collar. I stood with my feet apart to stand steady. The old woman was in my face. Looking at her now, she didn't seem as scary as she had before, but she was definitely ugly. Although I stand by the statement that she had never washed her hair, her entire body was wet. Her hair was dripping, and large gobs of water ran down her face and dripped off the end of her crooked nose. It was not raining.

"You don't have a bag, boy."

"No," was all I could say.

"Hmmm." She scratched her hairy chin. "Well, we can't have that, can we? I bet you had all sorts of lovely things in there. Your books and clothes and games, I'll bet. We'll have to do something about that, won't we?"

I tried to not answer the question. I looked at her and waited for her to move on to the next child, but she didn't. She kept looking. I noticed something weird about her eyes. Maybe it was just too dark, but I couldn't see the white bit. The whole of her eyes was a deep inky black.

"Yes," I said. "I guess so."

Slowly, her lips pulled up into a huge half-moon grin.

"You guess so? I guess so too."

She turned sharply to Mr Morris. "Show these to

their rooms. I'll get this one his things."

She grabbed my hand and pulled me into the hotel at a gallop. My elbow was sore where she'd yanked it. I was running to keep up with her.

"I bet you're tired."

"Yes. It was a long trip."

She nodded. "Brush your teeth and straight to sleep. You've got a big week coming." That grin again. "Right," she said. "Let's get you something to wear to bed."

She had stopped at a cupboard at the end of a dark corridor. She reached into her cloak and pulled out a long shiny key. She unlocked the cupboard and reached her bony hand in. I tried to get a glimpse inside, but she slammed the door shut. She was holding a set of ancient pyjamas. They were grey and all-in-one. I took them and felt the itch on my hands. The material felt like rough straw. It may have been the glimmer in the candlelight, but I thought I saw insects crawling around inside.

"Well," she said, staring.

"Well?"

"What do you say?"

"Oh! Thank you."

"Thank you, *Mrs Moon*..."

"Thank you, Mrs Moon."

Her smile quickly returned. "Right, let's get you a toothbrush."

She pulled me into a bathroom. There was no lock on the door and the entire floor was one big puddle. The toilet had a crack in the seat and the U-bend lay in the bath. Mrs Moon took a box off a shelf and pulled out a toothbrush. The toothbrush made the pyjamas seem posh. I wouldn't be surprised to learn that it was the first toothbrush ever invented. And that everyone who had ever been told off by the dentist had been made to use it as punishment and their plaque had never been cleaned off. I made a promise to myself that I would simply not brush my teeth for the remainder of this holiday.

Mrs Moon left the bathroom and stood in the corridor.

"You see those stairs, there? Up and to the left. That's the boys' room. Clean up and go to bed." She leaned in close. "Which direction did I say?"

"Up the stairs and to the left."

"Good. That's the boys' room. And what are you?"

"I'm a boy."

"Good. So, make sure you turn left. Goodnight." And she was gone.

I stood in the flickering candlelight holding my new pyjamas and toothbrush, wishing that I had my bag. I could've worn my own pyjamas. I would have called home too if I had my phone. I sighed. Then I heard something coming from behind me. A high-pitched whine like an animal in pain. I turned around and only saw the dirty bathroom. There was nothing in here.

"Jack!" Suddenly, I felt cold.

"Hello?" I asked.

"Jack! Come here!" It was a man's voice. I looked around the room and saw where it must be coming from. Right at the top of the far wall was a tiny window. I wondered if I'd be able to squeeze through it.

"Jack!" it went again. "Come here."

I threw my things down and tried to climb the toilet to get to the window. The crack in the toilet seat gave way and it snapped in two. I slipped, and my foot went into the toilet. I could feel my sock filling with cold water. I hoped it wasn't filling with anything worse.

Mrs Moon was at the door again.

"What the hell are you doing, boy?"

"I was just-"

"You're not here to cause trouble, you know."

"I wasn't causing trouble. Someone said my name, so I was trying to look-"

"That's quite enough of that."

She pulled me out and pushed me into the corridor. She threw the pyjamas and toothbrush at me.

"Upstairs and to the left," she said.

I could hear the water in my sock sloshing as I climbed the steps. At the top of the stairs was a corridor that ran in two directions: the left and the right. I peered down the right corridor, trying to catch a glimpse.

"To the left," she called from behind me.

Without looking back, I walked to the boys' bedroom.

DAY ONE

CHAPTER 4
The Girl and the Monster

On the first day of the holiday, we went to see Tintagel Castle. I was actually excited about that because Ruby had said how much she wanted to see it. I was disappointed to find out, however, that Ruby would not be coming.

"All the boys line up to get on the bus," shouted Mr Morris.

"Just the boys?" asked Thomas. "What are the girls doing?"

"The girls will be doing some activities with Lowenna today."

"Lowenna?" I asked.

"That'll be Mrs Moon to you. Anyway, boys. What the girls are doing today is none of your concern. Why are you not lining up to get on the bus?"

Some of the boys were grabbing their coats and bags. Thomas and I dawdled. Mr Morris clocked us and nodded towards the door. I picked up my book – my only possession now – and took a seat on the bus. The other boys were throwing things and running around. I sat towards the back and looked out of the window. I saw a truck pull up outside. A short, fat man in green overalls got out and carried a tray of fish to the hotel kitchen.

When we arrived, Thomas asked, "Is that it?"

Tintagel Castle looked really cool! It was in ruins. There were broken down halves of wall all over and I wondered how old they were. There was a long bridge that ran between two mountains. I wondered if I'd be able to sneak away and explore on my own. I was going to choose somewhere really cool to show Ruby later.

As Mr Morris was explaining that the castle was built during the Romano-British period, I grabbed my book and made my way down to the coast. I knew that there was a spot down there called Merlin's Cave. I didn't know if Merlin was a real person but I'd read stories about him so I wanted to check it out.

I saw a broken-down bit of wall with a gap in the middle – I imagined some Roman archer using it to watch for enemies. I decided I would sit down here and read my book. When the class had moved on, I would run down to Merlin's Cave. I found a dry patch and sat down.

When I'd finished the chapter, I checked through the wall crack. They were on the other side of the bridge now and Mr Morris was explaining something. Nobody seemed to notice I was missing. There were other people about now, looking around the castle. This was good. It would be easier for me to blend in.

I replaced my bookmark, stood up and made my way down the hill. I stopped when two figures caught my eye in the distance. There was a woman and a girl. They both looked small, but after a closer look, the woman was just hunched over. She was all in black and lent on a stick. *Could it be?*

The hunched woman grabbed the girl by the hair and plunged her into the sea. I couldn't believe what I was seeing. I jumped back in surprise. What was she doing? I saw the girl's two little hands grabbing up at the other's arm, but she clearly wasn't strong enough. The woman pulled her back up for a moment and then, with both hands, held her under for longer. They struggled. I don't know how long I was watching. It was all so shocking. Eventually, she stopped struggling and her body went still. I gasped. Was she dead? I thought she was.

The woman stood and put down her hood. I squinted and tried to see her face. She held the girl's body out with both her arms. And then it happened. It was like an the tentacle of an octopus. It was long, it was slimy, and it was purple. It rose slowly out of the water and uncurled, until it reached taller than the woman standing. The tentacle wrapped around the young girl's body several times and dragged her into the water.

Then I saw the woman's face, and I knew who it was. It was Lowenna Moon. I saw the hideous, wet wrinkled skin and the dirty knotted hair. Mrs Moon stood on the beach and watched the water settle and then, in one quick turn of the head, she looked directly at me.

I don't remember running away, but I remember reaching the class.

"Mr Morris! You've got to come stop it!"

"Shush, Jack! We're learning about King Arthur. Pay attention."

"Sir, you've got to come."

"Be quiet."

"Where were you?" said Thomas.

"I was down by the beach. I just saw this girl, and-"

"You were down by the beach?" Mr Morris asked. I thought his face looked scared. "What on Earth were you doing there?"

"I was just reading my book. But that's not the point. You have to listen to this. She killed her!"

Now all the boys were paying attention.

"Who's been killed?"

"A girl! It was Mrs Moon."

"Mrs Moon has been killed?" asked Thomas. "Cool!"

"Stop!" Mr Morris whispered this, but it was more frightening than if he'd shouted. His lips were thin. "Take me there."

We walked quietly to the wall where I had been reading. The boys followed in a line, whispering about what was going on. I picked my book up off the grass.

"You're a liar, Jack," someone shouted.

"Well, where is your drowned girl?"

"She was down there," I said, pointing to the spot. But she was gone. I didn't know whether to tell them about the creature. They wouldn't believe me. They would just think that I was crazy or telling lies.

"You should be ashamed of yourself, making up stories about Lowenna like that." *Lowenna.* "When we get back to the hotel, you're going to apologise to her."

As we rode back to the hotel, I wondered who the girl was, and I started to worry. What if it was Ruby, and that's why the girls hadn't come with us? I mean, Mrs Moon was staying with the girls so it must have been one of them. I wished again that I had my phone, so that I could check on Ruby.

I looked out of the rear window of the bus and down to the beach. I tried to see anything. People, a movement in the water, an eerie monstrous tentacle reaching from the depths. But we rounded a corner, and I saw nothing.

CHAPTER 5
<u>Don't Eat the Eyeballs</u>

I was very relieved to find Ruby alive and well when we got back to the hotel for lunch. The girls and the boys were back together and eating in the hotel dining room. Everything they served had come out of the ocean. Fresh crab, oysters, prawns. I carefully picked anything I could find that didn't still have the eyeballs attached and sat down, saving a space for Ruby.

"I know we're by the sea, but I thought they'd have something else, at least," she said as she sat down. She had a tuna sandwich on her plate.

"Hmmm?" I said. I wasn't really listening. I was looking at the dimple in her cheek as she grinned at me.

I'd told her all about what had happened at the beach. She was the only one that I dared tell the full story to. She didn't seem to think I was crazy, but she didn't think I'd really seen a monster either. I was starting to doubt it myself.

"You really didn't get a good look?" she asked.

"What?"

"At the girl?"

"Oh. No, not really. She was blonde, I think."

"And you think the woman was Mrs Moon?"

"I don't *think* she was Mrs Moon. It *was* Mrs Moon. She looked right at me."

"Okay," she said, holding up her hands because I had raised my voice. I hated being made to feel stupid or a liar. "Have you rung your parents to tell them you're here okay? I mean, did you ring your auntie and uncle?"

"How could I?" I asked, annoyed. "I lost my phone, didn't I?"

"I just thought Grace might call them for you. Isn't she…?"

"Oh, yeah." Why hadn't I thought of that? I could've kicked myself for being so stupid. Of course, Grace would be able to get in touch with them. "Do you know where she is?"

"Probably still with Thomas. Do you know where they went today?"

"What do you mean? Thomas was at Tintagel Castle with me."

"Oh." Ruby looked confused.

"What's going on, Ruby?"

"Well, nothing. Probably. Just that nobody saw Grace today. She was playing games with us in the hall, and then..." She thought for a moment. "Mrs Moon took her out to speak to her about something, and I think that's probably when I last saw her. Yeah, I think it was."

"And you haven't seen her since then?"

"Nobody has. Me and the girls were talking about it. It was weird, but we figured she must have just snuck off with Thomas. But he was with you?"

"Well, he was with us on the trip. I didn't see him when I was reading, but then he was with the group, and he was on the coach on the way back home."

"Oh? Weird." She went back to her food.

"Yeah, it was weird." I started to worry. "Hey, you don't think that Grace was the girl who got drowned, do you?"

"Don't be silly," she said, but she looked worried too.

"Where is Thomas?" I asked. "He's not in here."

She shrugged. "Gone back up to the boys' room?"

Something weird was going on and I wanted to find out what it was. I told Ruby that I was going to go check, and I left my food. I went to the boys' room. Up the stairs and to the left. I glanced to the right again, as I had the night before. I wondered if I would ever get to see what was down that corridor as the light at the end of it flickered. I remembered Mrs Moon standing at the bottom of the stairs, scolding me and telling me to go left. I swung round, expecting to see her standing down there, staring up at me with the cold eyes from back at the beach.

But she wasn't there. The corridor was empty. I carried on until I met the room I shared with Johnny – the kid with the PlayStation – Thomas, and the two brothers, Terry and Jerry. I could never remember which brother was which. I turned the heavy, rusty handle and opened the door. When I saw what was in the room, I jumped back and actually screamed. Thomas's body lay on his bed in a pile of blood. His eyes were crossed, and his tongue hung limply out of the side of his mouth.

CHAPTER 6
The Dead Boy who Screamed

I stepped closer to Thomas's corpse. The smell was horrible. I was so frightened. I had never seen a dead body before in my life and I hated that I was here on my own. I didn't know what you were supposed to do in a situation like this. Should I phone an ambulance? Or the police? Or is that just for when it's a murder? Then again, how did I know that this *wasn't* a murder? It looked pretty gruesome and there was blood everywhere. Was I supposed to give him mouth to mouth like they do in the movies? But I didn't know how to do that. Was I just supposed to blow into his mouth?

I lifted his hair out his face to get a good look at him. His eyes were closed. His tongue was dangling out of the side of his mouth and there was spit dangling off his chin. I got down on two knees to look really closely. With two fingers, I opened his eyes.

"Aaaaaarrrrgh!"

Thomas leapt up screaming like a maniac, and in his sudden movement, he headbutted me right on the nose.

"Ow!" I cried as I fell down onto my bum. I licked my lip, which felt wet, and I tasted blood. My nose burnt. He had broken my nose! "Ow, man!" I said again.

"Well, what did you get so close for?" he asked.

"Because I thought you were dead."

Thomas paused for a second and then he fell back down on the bed in a fit of laughter.

"You actually thought I was dead! I didn't even think it'd work but you fell for it! All of it! That was so funny! I could hardly keep it together!"

"It was not funny. I was really scared."

"You're such a baby."

"I'm not listening to you. I think you broke my nose."

"I did? Let me see." He looked at my face. "Oh my god! I did, didn't I! Hey, that hurt me too, you know. You've got some conk on you, mate."

"What am I supposed to do? Am I supposed to put my head back or forwards?"

"How the hell should I know? I look like a doctor to you?"

He didn't look like a doctor. He looked like a bloody murder victim who had just gotten up for one last fit of laughter.

"You're gonna be in so much trouble when they see the sheets, you know."

Thomas didn't care. He took his phone out and started playing a game. "Gives 'em an excuse to change 'em. They need changing. It was itchy in those sheets last night."

I shoved some toilet roll up each nostril and, not knowing if forwards or backwards was best, I tried to keep my head as level as it was humanly possible.

"You still here?" Thomas asked.

"I'm a bit busy trying to stop my head from bleeding out, actually," I said.

"Oh, stop it, you baby. It's a bit of blood. You've stopped now, anyway. Why don't you go?"

I nearly did go, but I remembered something. "Because I came up here to ask you a question."

"Oh yeah?"

"Have you seen Grace?"

"Is she that girl with blonde hair?" He grinned at me. I tried to look angry but it's hard to do that with toilet paper sticking out of your face. "No, I haven't seen her recently. Why?"

"What does recently mean?"

He sighed and said, "I haven't seen her today."

"All day? At all?" I started to panic.

"For god's sake. I just said that, didn't I? What's all this about?"

I cleared some space on the end of the bed and sat down. I pulled the toilet roll away to show that this was a very serious discussion. I put on my most grown up face as I told Thomas everything that had happened down at the beach that morning.

I waited a long time as he digested the news that I'd given him.

"You're an idiot," he said. "Or crazy. Probably both. You're telling me that the landlady fed your sister to a sea-monster?"

"My cousin."

"Look," he said. He closed the game on his phone and looked for Grace's number. "It's ringing." We waited, and there was no answer. "Well, it doesn't prove anything."

But he looked worried. "Why wouldn't she answer me? Is she annoyed at me or something?"

"I think it's more serious than that, Thomas."

"Shut up, you don't understand this stuff."

"What stuff?"

"Come on." He grabbed my arm and pulled me to the door. "We're going to try the girls' room. She'll be in there and we'll ask her why she's ignoring me."

"She's not there! I asked Ruby about it. She said none

of the girls have seen her all day."

That made him stop.

"Well… Look, I'm not saying I believe you. There's got to be a reason to all of this that actually makes sense. But just to be safe, I say that we go down to where you were this morning and we…"

"Investigate?"

"No, not investigate. Just sort of look around and see what clues we can find, you know."

I agreed, happy to be getting somewhere, and we left the boys' room. However, when we got outside, we saw that the corridors were not empty. Mrs Moon was patrolling and making sure that nobody was trying to do what we were doing – leaving the building.

We agreed that we would go the next day, when it was light, and we could have a proper look around.

When I went to the bathroom before bed, I heard it again.

"Jack! Jack!" The same voice, the same direction, coming from that small window at the top of the bathroom wall. Well, tonight I was sick of mysteries. I went back to the boys' room and pulled a big stack of the heaviest books I could find. I put the cracked toilet seat together and piled the books on top of it. I held on to the toilet and, as I climbed up, the books wobbled. I was able to just reach enough to peer throw the bottom of the glass, and I nearly fell.

It was him! The guy from the toilet at the service station. The guy who'd tried to kidnap me. The guy who'd taken my backpack.

He was waving it over his head. "Jack! Come with me! I've got your bag."

The books gave way beneath me and I fell to the floor. Ignoring the mess, the old pain in my nose and the new pain in my leg, I threw myself into bed and under the covers.

DAY 2

CHAPTER 7
<u>Mr Morris's Plans Ruined</u>

The rain was hitting the roof tiles so hard the next morning that it woke me up. I pulled the cover down from over my face and looked around the bedroom. Jerry, Terry and Johnny were sat on the floor playing a board game. Johnny's PlayStation lay unplugged on his bed because there was no television to attach it to. Thomas, however, was sat at the foot of the bed with his phone out. He just stared out at the rain running down the window.

"You okay, Thomas?"

"Huh? Oh, yeah. Your sister still isn't replying to my texts." He put it in his pocket. "So, I've been thinking. You might me right. About her. About something weird going on."

"I'm glad you agree. Should we go check it out?"

He nodded. "Let's go."

I went to the bathroom and tidied up the mess of books from the night before. Then I threw on my one set of dirty clothes, and we went down to the communal area for breakfast. Mr Morris and Mrs

Moon were watching out of the window. Mrs Moon looked a bit healthier today. Maybe I was imagining it, but she seemed to stand a bit straighter. She even looked a bit younger. I took a bowl and filled it with corn flakes. I left the bacon which was some light shade of blue. Thomas, unbothered, loaded four rashers onto a slice of bread and covered them in tomato ketchup.

Ruby came and sat with us. She had also decided to have corn flakes, I noticed.

"Still no sign of Grace," she said.

"She's not replying to my texts either," Thomas said.

"It's too weird," I added, feeling that I should say something important. "Listen, Ruby. Thomas and I think something's going on."

"Oh, something is definitely going on."

"So, we're going to head out of here after breakfast. We're going down to where I saw that girl get attacked, and we're going to look for clues."

"You sound like that guy from scooby Doo. What was his name?"

"Fred?" I loved Scooby Doo. I'd seen every episode. "But we're not going to split up. Bad things happen when you split up."

She smiled at me and said, "You're such an idiot." I smiled back.

"P'ah!" Thomas spat out raw bacon and chewed-up bits of bread. Thin lines of saliva ran from his lips to the sandwich. "There's something wrong with this bacon."

"Thomas! Were you listening?"

"Yeah, yeah. I was listening. I'm just saying. That was disgusting."

Our attention was broken as Mr Morris called for quiet. He looked like he was going to cry. Mrs Moon, on the other hand, was practically grinning. She looked around the room as though she'd just arrived at an all-you-can-eat buffet and couldn't decide what to eat first.

"I'm afraid, children, that this damnable British weather of ours has put a bit of a dampener on our plans today. As you know, we'd planned to go to the Tintagel Toy Museum. Well, I'm afraid that with the rain thundering down the way that it is, it is simply impossible for us to drive. So..." He wiped his eyes and forced a smile. "We're going to play some games here at the hotel. We're going to light all the big wooden fireplaces and make this place really cosy."

I doubted that the Moonlight Hotel had ever been cosy.

"And another thing," said Mrs Moon, standing tall. I could've sworn that her eyes flickered to me for half a second. "Before I go on, I want you all to know that you are perfectly safe here in my home." I exchanged a look with Ruby. "I should point out that this weather makes it dangerous for *anybody* to venture out, so it would be a very stupid thing if any little boy or girl tried to go outside. On another note, it has come to my attention that a strange man has been sighted loitering around outside this building. We don't know what he wants but he may start causing trouble. He has a long beard and wears thick black eyeglasses."

"Oh my god," I whispered.

"What?" said Thomas.

"I saw him."

"You're kidding!"

"I saw him last night, outside my window. It's that guy from the service station. The one who stole my bag."

Ruby covered her mouth. "That's so scary."

"He must have been going through my things too. He knew my name."

"Naturally, the police have been informed. He has not been seen today but that is likely due to the weather. This gentleman tends to stay around the boys' bedrooms and was caught yesterday trying to climb up to the bathroom window. He ran away before we were able to apprehend him. I don't wish to frighten you, children. I only tell you this so that you will understand why I am bringing in the following rule: until this man is caught, we are going to keep all of our doors and windows locked, day and night. The weather, today, stopped our plans anyway but I suggest you get used to entertaining yourselves inside, because until this man is caught, you cannot leave this hotel."

CHAPTER 8

<u>And then there were two...</u>

"Mrs Moon just means until the end of the week, doesn't she?" I asked.

"I don't think so," said Ruby. "I think she wants to keep us here for a very long time."

We had spent all day discussing how we were going to get out. We checked all the doors and windows in the hotel. They were all locked. Thomas was sure that he could pick the locks. Ruby was sceptical but he didn't get chance to find out. We spent a little too long looking at one door at the back of the kitchen when Mrs Moon came and saw us off.

We were sat in the dining room, planning what to do next. We knew that if we were going to do anything, we were going to need to wait until it went dark and everyone was in bed. We were sat around a small wobbly table in the corner with a little candle for light. Ruby had made three cups of coffee for us all to help us stay awake. I kept adding milk to mine to get rid of the taste. I wanted a Coke but that was too 21st century for this hotel. Ruby liked it. She was sat with her cup at her lips, deep in thought. Thomas twirled his spoon in circles, playing with it. Immediately, Ruby threw her cup down and slapped herself on the forehead.

"It's so simple!" she said.

"What is?" Thomas and I asked.

"The deliveries. They bring the fish in through the back to the kitchens. That's the only door they can't keep locked. What we've got to do is distract Mr Morris and then we'll be able to rush out of the door before he returns."

But it turned out that we didn't need to distract Mr Morris. He was stood by the door, biting his lip.

"Ms Davies?"

"Huh?" Thomas asked asked.

"Me," said Ruby.

"I think you'd better come with me."

The three of us looked at one another. I put my hand on Ruby's arm. I saw that Thomas had done the same. I didn't believe in psychic powers, but at that moment, I was trying my hardest to send the message to Ruby, *Do not go with him. He must have been listening.*

"And why is that?"

"I'd really rather not discuss it in front of the boys. Just come with me, Ms Davies."

"We're in the middle of a discussion. Can it wait?"

"For goodness' sake, Ruby," he said. "It's your grandmother.

"What?" She stood up.

"Yes," he said, nodding gravely. "Now you see why I didn't want to discuss this in front of... them. I have your mother on the phone. She wants to speak to you immediately."

Oh no, I thought. *Ruby loves her grandma.* But part of me didn't believe it. Thomas clearly didn't either. He was scowling at Mr Morris. Ruby, however, was crying. She patted me on the shoulder and ran out of the room. Mr Morris took a moment, before he left and looked at us both. I'm sure I saw it! Thomas isn't, but I'm convinced. As Mr Morris turned, he smirked at us. Then he closed the door behind him.

Thomas grabbed me quickly. "You know what that means. There's no one at the door."

"But what if he locked it before he came here?"

"There's only one way to find out. Let's go."

He jumped up and pulled me by my T-shirt. I wasn't sorry to leave the coffee behind. We looked both ways to see if anyone was looking and went to the delivery door.

It was open!

"But what about Ruby?"

"Oh, forget her! Let's go!"

The journey down to Merlin's cave was surprisingly easy. In fact, we were both so worried about Ruby and Grace that it was all kind of a blur. When I think back on it now, I vaguely remember jumping on a bus and heading down to the beach. Thomas had to pay because I had no money. Most of the people on there were in their twenties. There were lots of couples with their arms round each other, kissing. I think they were drunk.

We got off, and I led Thomas down to where I'd seen the girl drown. He took his phone out and used it as a torch. I put my hand in my pocket. I groaned as I remembered that my phone was gone. I hated not having my phone.

"So where was it?"

"It was just around here. There, where the water comes up. That woman was stood here." I shuddered as I remembered her looking up at me. "Mrs Moon. I'm sure it was her."

"You mean *Lowenna*," Thomas said and sniggered.

"Yeah. Lowenna." I laughed too.

"Wait!" Thomas jumped down on his knees. "Look at this. Here, take the phone. Shine it on this." He scrambled in the sand and dug something out.

"What is it?"

"Look at this!" he said and held it out.

"So, it *was* her."

He handed me Grace's bracelet.

"She always wears it," Thomas said. "Oh my god, man. What's going on? Why would someone do that to her? What is this place?"

But I didn't have time to respond because a hand grabbed me around the neck.

CHAPTER 9
The Two Strange Glowing-Egg-Eyed Boys

The hand around my neck belonged to Mr Morris. He wasn't trying to strangle me, but he certainly wasn't trying to give me a cuddle either. His short hands were gripping the best they could, and his fingertips were digging into my neck. Even today, when it gets cold, the marks of fingernails show up in blue on my skin.

"What the hell do you think you're doing?"

I'd love to tell you that it was me who said that. I'd be justified in asking that of a teacher grabbing me around the neck in the middle of the night after a series of mysterious events. But it wasn't me who said it. It wasn't Thomas. It wasn't even Mr Morris. It was two people in fact. The two brothers from our room stood behind Mr Morris. Their names were Jerry and Terry, but I could never remember which was which. They had the same hair and were the exact same height. Today though, there was something else that was strange and similar about them. They had the same eyes. It was the most obvious thing in the pitch blackness of the cave. They had big glowing eyes that never seemed to blink. Like two glow-in-the-dark eggs floating in the darkness.

They spoke again, at completely the same time: "Thomas and Jack, you are being bad. What are you doing here?"

I was speechless. Thomas tried to throw a rock at them but missed. "As if! I bet you two grassed on us. Haven't you got anything better to do?"

Thomas's outburst seemed to remind Mr Morris of where he was and what he was doing. He let go of my neck, and I gasped for breath. "You boys are in so much trouble, you have no idea. What on earth did you think you were doing here?"

"We know what you did!" I shouted.

"Yeah," said Thomas. "We've got-" I shook at my head at him. I didn't think it was right to tell any of these people about the bracelet. Not yet, at least.

"You've got what?" said Mr Morris.

"What have you got?" asked Jerry and Terry, together.

"We've got to find my girlfriend," said Thomas. I heard the boys snigger.

"Grace, he means," I said. "My cousin is missing."

"Oh boys."

"Boys, boys, boys," added the boys.

"Boys", continued Mr Morris. "Miss Williams is back at the Moonlight Hotel. She's rather under the weather, I'm afraid, and has spent the day in bed. That's why you won't have seen her. You can't go in the girls' room. I'm so sorry that you were both worried about her. I suppose I ought to have explained the situation better so that nobody worried. I didn't consider how close your expanded family is, Jack. And Thomas, I didn't realise that the two of you were an item. I considered you too young, to be totally honest. But kids today. Would you both like to come back to the hotel with me and see how Grace is doing?"

I didn't believe a word of it. If Grace had spent all day in bed, then why didn't Ruby know where she was? No, there was more to this than met the eye.

I glanced over at Thomas. He was hard to read in the dark, but I didn't think that he'd bought a word of this rubbish either.

Jerry and Terry still hadn't blinked once. They looked at me, to Thomas, and back to me.

"That's not true," I blurted out.

The calm smile on Mr Morris's face momentarily gave way. It returned just as quickly and he asked through gritted teeth, "What do you mean, that's not true? Do you know something that I don't?"

"We asked Ru- We asked one of the girls to look for Grace for us. They said that they hadn't seen Grace either. All day. So, she can't have just been in bed."

Mr Morris seemed to be chewing on this piece of information for a long time. The boys continued to stare, unnervingly.

"My my, you have done your homework on this one."

The boys sniggered.

"But the fact of the matter is that she is at the hotel right now and you would see this to be true if you would just follow me." He sighed when we didn't move. I gripped the bracelet in my fist. "Okay, you want the whole truth? The fact of the matter is that Miss Williams *has* been missing today but is now returned to us. We don't know where she has been. She hasn't told us. She does seem very unwell indeed. We didn't think it right, Lowenna and I, to push her too hard. We're going to let her rest tonight, and we'll ask all the relevant questions tomorrow, if she's feeling better. I would advise you two to follow the same tactic."

Apparently satisfied with his explanation, Mr Morris turned on his heel and called over his shoulder, "Come on then, If you want to see your cousin – and girlfriend."

We started walking but Terry and Jerry took our arms, one each, and escorted us both back up the hill to the hotel. It would've looked to a stranger like we were being arrested. That's how it felt to us too.

CHAPTER 10
The Things that Live in the Dark

"Is she dead?" I asked when I saw Grace's white, still, clammy body on the bed. Her face was turned away from us.

I poked at her arm. She turned her head lazily in our direction and pulled in a pained breath.

"No," said Mr Morris, with a smirk.

"Obviously not," said Terry. I knew it was Terry because when we had reached the hotel, Mr Morris had turned to the boys and said, "Jerry, take Thomas to the kitchen. He can wait. I'll entertain Jack's idiotic concern because he is Grace's family, but none of this boyfriend-girlfriend nonsense. Not at your age. I'll deal with him afterwards." And the boy who must have been Jerry took Thomas down the hall.

Terry's bulging eyes were still staring. However, it didn't look as creepy now that we were in the light. It just looked ridiculous. But he wasn't the only one. When Grace turned to face me, I saw that she had the same glowing egg-like eyes. I could have believed that she didn't have any eyelids.

"What happened to you?"

Grace took another pained breath. Her chest went up an inch and back down as she struggled for breath. But before she could answer, Mr Morris put his hand on my shoulder and brought me out of the room. "Okay, you've seen that she's alive. Will you put this ridiculous conspiracy to bed?"

It was dark now and I made to head up to the boys' bedroom. I wanted to see what had happened to Thomas.

"I haven't dismissed you, Jack."

Ugh. I turned around.

"What?"

"Come with me."

He led me down the stairs and towards the dining room. We stopped at the table where we'd made our escape plan. It seemed so long ago now. Our cold coffee was still there.

"Sit down."

"What?"

"I said... Sit."

I sat. I didn't want to. I was very angry, very cold and very confused. But the grown-up told me to sit down, so I sat down.

"What on earth did you think you were doing out

there tonight, Mr Williams?"

"I told you."

"You've told me. Oh yes, you've told me. But what if I don't believe this ridiculous story that you've told me?"

I shrugged. He walked to the window and began closing the blinds.

"The sea is dangerous. You must respect it. You ran off tonight. I thought that incident with the gentleman who took your bag would have put a healthy dose of fear into you. And you wandered off today at Tintagel Castle too! Frankly, I'm appalled that you chose to go out on your own tonight."

"I wasn't alone," I countered. "Thomas was with me."

He laughed. "Thomas! Oh yes, what help a twelve-year-old boy was going to be against a murderer or a wild beast. Or a sea monster! You have no idea what lurks in the dark. I've been coming here a lot longer than you've been alive and even I don't know it all." He leaned close to my face. "There are scarier things that live in the dark than you can imagine, Jack Williams."

I didn't want to show that he was actually creeping me out. I swallowed to make sure that my voice would come out clearly. "So, can I go?"

"You may go to your bedroom soon – after I've

spoken to your friend Thomas and when I choose to head up for the night. Tomorrow, and for the rest of the trip, you can both consider yourselves grounded. You will not leave the hotel until the end of the week. You will stay within my sight and will not leave any room unless *I* give you express permission. I will be informing both of your parents what you have been doing-"

"She won't care." Thomas was stood in the doorway. "I'll be surprised if my mum even answers the phone."

Mr Morris rose. He seemed much taller now than I'd ever noticed him be before. "Jack, you may go to bed now. Leave me to... deal with Thomas."

DAY THREE

CHAPTER 11
<u>How Do You Catch a Fish?</u>

The rain didn't let up the next day. The sound of the rain bashing off the roof was so loud that I was surprised the ceiling didn't fall in on us. I still hadn't seen Ruby since she had gone off to "answer her phone call". Thomas was too distracted with worrying about Grace. As for Grace…

She wasn't doing well.

Right now, she was lying in her bed, and we were trying to get some sense out of her. Mr Morris had finally allowed us to come up to see her when he saw how worried we were, but he was sat in the stiff wooden chair by the door. Grace was sticky with sweat.

"Argh!" Her tongue rolled backwards in her mouth as she moaned, which she was doing a lot of.

"What is it, Gracie?" Thomas asked.

Mr Morris coughed. "Miss Williams is suffering from a cold, of course. She was wandering out on the beach last night and was caught adrift in the water. She is lucky that we managed to find her. This habit of wandering off seems to be an epidemic and needs to be nipped in the bud."

Grace wouldn't - or couldn't? - shut her eyes but I saw that there were no pupils. Nothing looking out. I imagined her pupils on the back off her eyes, staring into her skull. Could she see her brain? I supposed it was probably too dark to see anything.

Mr Morris jumped up, and I know that because he knocked over his chair doing so.

"Lowenna!" he called.

Ugh. I turned round. Mrs Moon was stood in the doorway, her hand resting on the doorknob. Mr Morris was on the floor, picking up the mess he'd made.

Mrs Moon smiled at him the way someone would if they were mildly amused by a cat playing with a piece of string. Then she turned to us and her face became sad.

"I'm so sorry about the dreadful weather, children. Alas, I cannot control everything that happens around here."

"We're a little more concerned with my cousin's health at the moment."

"Ah, yes. The sleepwalker. Well, bad things happen to little boys and girls who wander off. Much like yourselves, I daresay. I am aware that you, yourself, wandered off at Tintagel Castle. It must run in the genes, I suppose."

Grace winced. Thomas apologised and let go of her hand. He put his hand on her arm gently.

"Anyway, children. I suppose you must all be bored inside playing board games. So, I've arranged something very special for you."

"What?" I asked.

"Lowenna," said Mr Morris, standing. "You didn't tell me anything about this."

"Hush, Stephen." Mr Morris sat. "Now, let's get you all out of this hotel. I know it's rather rustic. Nothing like what you kids want. So, I've spoken to my good gentleman friend, who's a fisherman." Mr Morris seemed to look up at her sadly. "He's agreed to take a group of children out into the sea and see how he catches the lovely fish that we've been enjoying. What do you say to that?"

"I say yes!"

It was Grace who said this. I wouldn't say that colour came back to her because it certainly didn't, but she did gain some energy and sit up. Her eyes were rolling about lazily in her sockets, but she seemed to have regained some control of her tongue and she was grinning.

"Let's do it! Let's get out on the waters."

I was really worried, and I tried to show this, with a look, to Thomas. Thomas, however, was grinning widely and grabbing Grace's hand. "Gracie! You're feeling better!"

"But won't a boat be dangerous in this weather?" I asked.

Thomas pushed me off the bed with a shove and said, "Oh, shut up, idiot. If Grace is up for it, then I'm game."

"Oh, I'm afraid not, Mr Roberts," said Mr Morris. "No, I'm afraid that your mum and dad are not happy with you."

"My mum *and* my dad?"

"Oh, yes. When I told him about your little excursion, your father was furious."

"That doesn't make any sense. My dad is dead."

Mr Morris wasn't listening. "He has demanded that we send you back home immediately. So, I suggest that you stop tugging at Miss Williams's arm like a Christmas cracker and that you make your way upstairs to pack your bags. You'll be leaving this afternoon."

Thomas looked at me. He looked scared.

"I suggest you do as your told, young man," said Mrs Moon. "I'm sure Grace and Jack will get on just fine without you. It will be a fun family adventure. What do you say?"

I looked at Grace. She started laughing.

CHAPTER 12
<u>Playing Games with the Fish-Boy</u>

I was starting to feel really gross wearing the same clothes. To be honest, it didn't stink that bad, but I was very aware that I couldn't get changed. I dreaded to think how it would be when my auntie picked me up stinking at the end of the week. All things considered, I was probably lucky to not have my mobile phone. Only two days into the holiday, it seemed like anyone who went to take a phone call disappeared around me.

I was sat in the main lobby of the hotel when I realised that I hadn't seen Ruby for a full twenty-four hours. The main lobby was a large, draughty room that was entirely made of wood. There were terrifying paintings on the wall that I assumed were of the Moon family. They all had thin, bony faces and whiteless eyes. The chairs, stiff and uncomfortable, had been pushed to the walls so that we could "play party games", as Mrs Moon put it.

These party games would have been boring even if we had been five-year olds, rather than twelve-year olds. We were playing pass-the-parcel at the moment, but as this game had been prepared at the last minute, the prizes were things that had been found around the hotel. Terry or Jerry had opened the parcel to find a whole haddock, head and everything. Strangely, he seemed delighted with it.

The music stopped when I was holding the parcel. I ripped off the last bit of newspaper without any enthusiasm. It was a toothbrush. But then I realised, it was *my* toothbrush. This was the grimy green thing with bristles missing that Mrs Moon had given me on the first day. I smiled weakly and, as I did, Mrs Moon stared right at me. I felt a shiver as I pictured her going through my things.

Looking around the room, I saw that I was one of the few children to not be having fun. In fact, most of the children were bobbing up and down to the beat of the music and clapping. Grace was joining in enthusiastically. She was cheering and whooping. Her thick, round eyes swelled with each up-and-down bob. Her hair was still greasy with sweat. Her face was still sticky and appeared to be starting to swell. Her lips had blown up like a fish's. But between those ballooned lips, it was clear that she was smiling.

Thomas and Ruby were nowhere to be seen. I wanted my phone when I thought of that. How easy it would have been to ring them and find out if they were okay. I wondered what had happened to Grace and wanted to find the others before the same thing happened to them.

"Yuck!"

A huge gob of something that was between spit and sweat dripped into my open palm.

"What are you doing!?"

I looked up and saw a boy grinning at me with his hands outstretched. His fingers had webs between them. A thin line of drool was running from his bottom lip. I scooted back to get out of its firing line. His face was just like Grace's, his lips bulging and fish-like. His lidless eyeballs throbbed and there were no pupils to show where he was looking. He was grinning though, and I knew he was grinning right at me.

I looked around the room to see if I was crazy or if everyone else was reacting the same way that I was. What I saw was horrifying. The whole room was like this. Okay, I wasn't, Mr Morris wasn't, and Mrs Moon wasn't. But everyone else was, all the children. Every grinning face in the room was swollen, sweaty and dripping.

"I need to get out of here," I cried and stood up.

My path was blocked by Mr Morris.

"Where do you think you're going? We're about to play wink murder."

Mr Morris had been following me everywhere all day. I had no chance of getting away without him watching, unless...

"I need to go to the bathroom."

He seemed to weigh this up in his mind. He knew what I knew: that he couldn't follow me into the bathroom. That's why I'd said it. I was going to head down the corridor and make a dash for it as soon as I turned the corner.

"Come on then," he said.

"What? You can't come to the toilet with me."

"I'll wait outside the door. Let's get going."

Oh no! What do I do now?

"Hurry up." He marched quickly down the corridor. I had no choice but to go to the toilet. Maybe I'd be able to squeeze out of the window, I wondered.

We reached the door to the boys' bathroom. Mr Morris leaned on the wall facing the door with his arms crossed.

"Be quick."

He'd got me. There was nothing I could do. I pushed the door open and walked in.

The lights were turned off and I was plunged into darkness when I got in. I felt for a light switch on the wall, but when I pressed it, nothing happened. I flicked it up and down, but the lights didn't come on. I reached out to feel my way.

"Ow!" I walked into a bin and hit my leg on it. I swore and rubbed my shin where it hurt.

And then I stood completely still. Because I heard crying come from somewhere in the room.

CHAPTER 13

<u>Jack Williams's First Kiss</u>

I pushed open the cubicle door.

"Hello," I called out with my open hand outstretched.

"Jack? Is that you?" It was Ruby! I couldn't see her, but I recognised her voice.

"Yeah, it's me."

"Oh, I'm so glad you're here, Jack! I don't know what's happening to me." I heard her sobbing.

"Ruby, where were you? I couldn't find you and I got really scared."

"I'm scared too! There's something really weird about this place. I don't like it. I want to go home!"

This is it, I thought. *My chance to be the hero.*

"Okay, let's remain calm," I said, "and figure this out. Where have you been for the last day?"

"I'm so sorry Jack! I'm sorry I left you."

"That's okay. Just try to breath. What did your mum say?"

"My mum? When?"

"When-" I felt awkward. "When she rang you about your grandmother."

"I don't know what you're talking about Jack."

"Last night. Mr Morris, he said-" I stepped closer.

Suddenly, I was struck by how close we were in this confined space. I could just about make her out now. Her face was so close to mine. Suddenly, all I could think of was kissing her on her lips. I couldn't see them now, but her lips looked so soft and pink all the time. My mouth felt so dry. I licked my lips and swallowed.

"Jack." She said my name slowly like she was hungry.

I heard Mr Morris bang on the door. "Hurry up."

"Jack. I want you to kiss me. I need you." *Oh my god.* I couldn't believe she was really saying it. "Please," she said. "Come here and kiss me." I stepped closer, trying to see where she was in the dark. I didn't want to miss, or to accidentally headbutt her. My heart was pounding through my chest. My stomach was full of butterflies.

The door banged again.

"Ignore him, Jack. I need you to kiss me. I need you now."

I leaned in and puckered my lips the way I'd seen people do it in movies. It was happening. This was my first kiss. I didn't care about all the horrible things that had happened on this holiday, just for this to happen now.

We kissed.

It wasn't what I had expected. Her lips were full the way I had always imagined them, but it was wetter than I had thought it would be. In fact, I was actually a bit disappointed. It felt kind of gross. Her nose felt sticky against mine, and I could feel the wet running down my forehead. I opened my eyes, and now I could see. Her eyes were wide open and glowing. They were bulging and they lit up everything else. Her lips were not full, as I had thought, but horribly swollen and fish-like. Her hair was thick and grimy.

I pulled back and screamed, but she grabbed onto me. "No, Jack. Don't go."

"Aargh." I tried to turn and open the cubicle door. She was surprisingly strong and held me in place. She leaned in, pushing her bloated lips at me. "Kiss me, Jack. Kiss me."

"No," I cried. I pushed at her sticky arms and was able to get away. I backed off and felt the wet strands of something gross connecting us. I grabbed onto the door to the bathroom and I felt her reaching around my neck. I pulled the door wide open and flung the pair of us out into the corridor.

Mr Morris stood up tall and looked momentarily shocked to see the pair of us emerge like that. Then he said, "Ah, Ruby. There you are. Anyway, come along you two. The group is waiting for us. I think Lowenna wants to play Friends and Foes next."

In the light of the candles that were scattered around the lobby, it was clear that Ruby and Grace were the same. The webbed fingers. The bulging eyes. I noticed something now that I hadn't seen before. They both had lines on their necks. They had rows of three flaps on their neck. They were like those gills that fish have to help them breath under water. I noticed them on Ruby first because she was sat next to me, but when I glanced over at Grace, I saw that she was the same. In fact, most of the children were the same. I could see that there were only a few kids that still looked like me. They had worried faces and were clearly checking out the room like I was. Johnny looked right at me. I tried to communicate with him without speaking. But what could I say? "Everything is going to be okay"? I didn't know that. "I've got a plan"? I wish.

Ruby was sidling closer to me and she tried to hold my hand. Defensively, I shoved my hands in my jacket pocket so that she couldn't get to me. I wondered where Thomas was and if there was any way I could contact him. I felt Grace's bracelet in my pocket. I had picked it up after Thomas left to pack. I ran my fingers over the beads in thought.

I looked at Grace's arms and a chill ran through me. She was still wearing her bracelet! What did that mean?

I pulled the bracelet out of my pocket and checked it. It was definitely hers. She always wore it. It was the same one that Thomas and I had found at the beach. And yet, there it was around her wrist, exactly the same. Something was certain. The children sat around the room with me were not who I thought they were.

CHAPTER 15
<u>Receiving Texts from Nobody</u>

That evening, we were told to go to our rooms and change for the boat trip. We were told to dress as warmly as we could and wrap up in big, water-proof coats and to leave any electronic devices back in the hotel. All these gross fish-children were buzzing with excitement. Even I was a little excited because Mr Morris had left me alone while he made preparations with Mrs Moon. I even hoped that I would be able to catch Thomas packing in our room and say goodbye before he left.

But Thomas wasn't in our room. In fact, there was no trace of him. His bags had gone. His bed was made. Someone had obviously changed the bedding because the fake blood from his prank was gone too.

In contrast to all these things that were gone, something new had appeared. My backpack – the one that had been stolen - was on my bed. My heart jumped. I unzipped it. Everything was there. My clothes, my toothbrush, everything. My phone!

I pulled out my mobile phone and switched it on. My foot tapped the floor impatiently as I waited for it to load. I looked around and saw that the boys in the room were looking at me. There were three other boys in the room, now that Thomas was gone. Jerry and Terry had been fully fishified – for lack of a better word. They were watching me with interest. Johnny – who still seemed normal – was choosing clothes for the boat trip. Coat hangers rattled in his hand because he was shaking.

Feeling uncomfortable, I took my bag into the bathroom to get away from their stairs. I saw now that my phone had been fully charged. I started typing her a text:

> Aunt Sarah! Cant talk now but u've got 2 help me! Something really weirds going on. Think theyv got Grace. Gonna try to save her but u've got to help. Love u! Xxx

I was going to put the phone away when I spotted that I had a draft message. I hadn't written it. I clicked on it.

> Jack. Trust nobody. Meet me out front @18:00. Delete this message.

What? Who the hell had written that?

The phone rang. I jumped. It was Sarah. Yes! I was finally going to sort this.

"Hey! Thank god-"

"Now, you listen to me, young man! Your uncle and I are trying to have a relaxing holiday, but you have made this impossible. We don't understand why you two can't just get along."

"But, listen-"

"No, Jack. You listen to me. We've had to cut this trip short." *Yes! They're going to fix this. They're going to demand that Mr Morris and Mrs Moon explain themselves.* "We're driving up to your hotel. We're going to pick you and Grace up and we're going to drive straight home."

"You're what?"

"You heard. Not only are you ruining my holiday, but also the holiday of all those other poor kids in your class. Don't you think that they deserve some time off?"

"But-"

"I'm going to call your teacher and then we're going to come for you first thing in the morning."

She hung up.

I couldn't believe it. I was totally alone. Nobody believed me. My friends had disappeared. And my auntie was coming to take me away. Me and that thing that was pretending to be Grace. And who knew where the real Grace was? But if I didn't get her back soon, she'd be left here, and nobody but me would know that something was wrong. I couldn't let that happen. I needed a plan to rescue her. I needed to rescue Grace, Ruby and Thomas and I had to do it all by myself.

I knew I needed to get out of there. I needed to find out what had happened to Grace down at the beach. That was the answer to everything. I'd go down to where we'd found the bracelet and look for answers there. I was glad to have my phone back, but I wasn't ready to start trusting the weirdo who'd given it back to me. I mean, how did he even get in our room?

I went back into the boys' room. Everyone had changed into their raincoats and was grinning, ready for the boat trip. The boat trip! There was no way I could be left alone out there with these freaks. What would they do to me out there? Would they make me into one of them? I shuddered at the thought of what that process would look like.

They watched my every move. Two boys sat by the door, their expressions blank. Just making sure that I didn't make a run for it. I decided that if I was going to survive this, I would just need to go along with things for now. I pulled my clothes out of my bag and got changed. I put on a thick woollen hat and a big scarf and then I threw on my raincoat. The fish-boys were both grinning and chuckling quietly to themselves. It grew louder. It felt and sounded as though one person was laughing through two mouths.

The two fish boys at the door stood up. They approached me and Johnny.

"What are you doing?" he cried.

A slimy, scaly arm slid under my armpit and took control of me. We were being escorted out of the room. It was just like at the beach, only now Terry and Jerry were much stronger. I had to walk quickly just to keep pace with them.

There was a low rhythmic chuckle in their throats as they marched us down the corridor. I could see the gills on their neck flickering with each exhalation. My arm felt grimy and sticky. They stopped in the main lobby in front of Mrs Moon. Whereas she had looked so strong before, she now looked older and weaker than I had ever seen her. She stood in front of the front entrance, leaning on her stick for support. Her hands wobbled and I wondered if she was going to fall over. I decided I wouldn't help her up if she did.

She took a moment to find her breath. Then she said, "I'm afraid, children, that the boat ride will not be happening this evening." She wiped her eyes Her hands shook with anger. She gripped her stick in a tight fist and I could see her knuckles turning white. "Some... Someone... Some monster has sabotaged my good friend's boat and left it unable to sail. Until this heinous culprit has been caught, none of you will be going anywhere."

CHAPTER 16

The Interrogation

If I had thought that Mrs Moon was angry about what happened to the boat, it was nothing compared to Mr Morris. A selection of pupils was called into his room for angry questioning until he could get to the bottom of this. He did not say it, but I couldn't help noticing that the children who were investigated were all the ones who were still normal – us precious few.

Next, it was my turn. I saw a boy – I didn't know his name – coming out of Mr Morris's bedroom. He was rubbing his wrist and crying. He looked up, saw me and wiped his face.

"How was it?" I asked. He just shook his head and kept walking. Mr Morris appeared in the doorway. Normally, he would have shouted or at least scolded me. Now, he just looked and nodded his head to tell me to come in. I found it more frightening than if he had shouted. I stepped nervously into the room.

"Would you like to tell me what happened to the boat?" he asked, when I sat down.

"I don't know, sir."

"Are you sure about that?"

"Yes, sir."

"Well, I'm not so sure. I couldn't help but notice a lack of enthusiasm about this boat trip. How do I know that you didn't sabotage the boat in order to stop it from going ahead?"

"I wouldn't do that." I wished I had.

"That remains to be seen. You've done a lot of things on this holiday that I wouldn't have expected of you."

"Sir?"

"Yes, Mr Williams."

"Where is Thomas?"

He didn't hide his annoyance at all. "Thomas has been collected by his parents and has concluded his holiday early, as you well know."

"I didn't notice them arrive."

"They just left. You must have missed them."

"Don't you mean just his mum? Thomas's dad is dead."

He pushed on, ignoring this comment. "In fact, I received a rather exasperated phone call from your mother this evening. It appears that you too, will be going home. She's not happy with you."

"I'm surprised *my auntie* didn't decide to come get me when you rang her about me wandering off," I said.

He raised one eyebrow. I knew for certain that he'd never contacted any of our parents. And that made things even scarier. Where *had* Thomas gone?

"It is not for you to worry about the decisions of grown-ups. As a child, your job is to do as your told, and since you're struggling to achieve that one little task, I would advise you not to worry too much about what everyone else is doing with their time. Now, I want to ask you one more time. What did you do to the boat?"

"I didn't do anything to the stupid boat! I don't even know where it is."

I expected him to shout at me for raising my voice. Instead, he smiled. "Well, that's good. For your sake. Because I will be conducting a full inspection of the boat when I have concluded my questioning. And if I find *anything-*" He said the word "anything" very slowly. "-you *will wish* that you had told me the truth. That'll be all. Off you go."

I left the room with more questions buzzing around my head than ever before. There was so much about this place that I needed to learn and fast, but I felt like I understood none of it.

I had learnt one thing though. Mr Morris was going to be busy for a while conducting interviews.

Which meant that if I was going to slip out of the hotel, it needed to be right now.

CHAPTER 17
The Ruins of the Boat

Things almost went too easily. Mr Morris was too busy all evening to even notice me sneaking around. I expected that Mrs Moon would be keeping an eye on things. Nope. She was nowhere to be seen. In fact, I noticed, as I made my way carefully to the front entrance, that nobody was around. The entire hotel was eerily quiet. The windows showed that it was dark outside, and the flickering shadows left by the candles put me on edge. The door was unlocked. Things almost went too easily.

Almost.

As soon as I turned the handle, the front door swung wide open and slammed. I was sprayed with rain, and the wind was deafening.

"They were going to take us on a boat in this?"

In my whole life, I'd never seen a storm like it. I could even see panels of wood flying off the hotel. The front door swung back and forth on the hinge. The screws were coming loose. I gripped my coat tightly around my chin and ran out into the chaos.

I took the path that ran directly down to the coast. I could see a boat docked by the beach. I guessed that it was the one that we were heading out on later. The path was covered in mud. My foot gave way and I slid. I tried to grip onto anything. The wet mud was cold on my hands, but there was nothing solid to grip onto. My bum hurt where I landed. I stuck my feet out and managed to stop but was thrown forward onto my knees.

My hair was flat and wet on my face. I wiped water out of my eyes. I gripped my coat tighter around myself and headed up to the boat. The damage to it was obvious but whether it had happened during the storm or before was impossible to say. As I looked at it, I wondered how Mrs Moon could be so sure that a person had done this.

The entire side of the boat that was facing me was bare. I could see the inside, now soaked. There were a few small chairs around a table. There was a section at the front with the boat's wheel. The whole thing looked cramped and uncomfortable. I grabbed onto a part of the wall that was hanging open and pulled myself onto the boat. I looked around the cramped little chairs and imagined sitting here among the freakish fish kids. I pushed through the door and looked around the captain's section. I didn't know what you called a person who drove such a little boat. I guessed it was probably still a captain. I pulled open drawers. I didn't know what I was looking for. Anything, I guess. Any sort of clue to the mystery that I was living through.

"What's this?"

There was a small compartment, just under the wheel. I would've missed it if I hadn't been so frantically pulling at anything. It came open, and inside, I found a little wooden chest. There was a thick padlock lock on the clasp. I gave it a shake. It rattled.

Suddenly, I became aware of a big black shape through the window. I wiped at the window and tried to make sense of it. There was a huge group of people out in the storm that was getting closer. I put the box in my coat pocket and climbed out of the boat.

When I landed on the ground, I spotted another similar black mass from the rear of the boat. I saw what it was. My classmates – or some hideous imitation of them – marching towards me in their black winter coats. They didn't seem as bothered by the weather as I was. They simply walked along calmly. I turned back to the shape I'd seen at the front of the boat. Another group of children was heading to me from that direction. This group was led by a slightly taller figure. Mrs Moon was walking along using her stick and leading the group. She was walking tall now. They were closing in on me. This was it. They had caught me. They were closing in on me from all sides and they were going to turn me into one of them, drown me, feed me to a sea monster. I didn't know what they were going to do but it wasn't going to be nice.

I looked at the slope up to the hotel. I had no chance of climbing up that with the mud running down it. And even if I did, where would I go? They'd just follow me back to the hotel – if it was still standing – and then I was stuck.

I looked to the sea. It was ridiculous, but my only option seemed to be to swim away. It was that or wait and be captured. I took a breath, and prepared to jump in.

I heard a huge, rumbling growl from behind me. Someone, driving a dirty, blue car, came speeding down the muddy path. At first, I was scared that it was going to run into me, but then, the driver turned, hit the brakes, and sprayed mud all over Mrs Moon and her gang of children.

"Jack! Get in, now!"

The door pushed open. Without any other options, I jumped inside.

CHAPTER 18
<u>The Madman's Tale</u>

The car sped off. The engine growled with the strain and we nearly drove into Mrs Moon and her followers. They had to jump to get out of the way. We sped up the hill and onto the road. I pressed my face up against the window trying to catch a glimpse of what was going on, but in the rain and wind, it was impossible to see anything.

"You were lucky I was there!" said the driver in a grumpy voice. "That place is crazy, and that school is crazy for bringing kids here."

"This whole thing is crazy!" I shouted. My heart was pounding. I was so frightened.

"Well, I've got you now, kid," he said. He shook my knee and I pulled away.

When I had gotten into the car, I hadn't had time to notice who my rescuer was. All I knew was that I was in danger, and he was offering me an escape. But now that I was out of danger and had time to look carefully, I knew exactly who he was. This was the man at the service station who'd taken my bag and tried to kidnap me. This was the man who'd been stalking the hotel and calling my name up through the bathroom window.

"It's you."

He smirked. "I guess it must be."

"You put my bag in my room."

"I did. Did you delete the text?"

"How did you get in there?"

"Please. The locks in that place are too simple. Do you really think that monster *wants* to stop people getting in? Or for them to get out?" He looked at me and raised an eyebrow.

"What's going on? Who are you? Why are you trying to help me when you were going to kidnap me before?"

"What? Kid, are you crazy? Did they tell you I was kidnapping you? I was saving you. If I'd have succeeded, you'd never gone to that evil place." He looked at me hard, even though the car was going really fast. "Show me your neck."

"What?"

"Your neck! Show it me, now."

"What are you going on about?" I asked but I pulled my collar down anyway.

"Hmm." He shrugged, unconvinced.

He turned off the road and onto a part of beach enclosed by two hills. I immediately recognised where we were. This was Merlin's Cave. I thought about everything that happened on this trip so far, and how I'd seen Mrs Moon drowning a girl here. I decided it probably was Grace. My legs felt weak. The man opened the door, climbed out, and walked into the cave. I jumped out to follow him.

"Are you going to explain what's going on?" It was quieter in here. The storm couldn't reach inside the cave, but still, the wind echoed off the walls like a wailing ghost.

He pulled out a torch, said, "Just keep up and listen," and carried on.

I walked two steps for every one of his to keep up.

"I grew up in Tintagel. I've lived here all my life, and I know all about the Moonlight Hotel. I even stayed there once when I was a little boy."

"It looks old enough."

"Believe me, it looked that way when I was there too. Anyway, a group of friends and I went out surfing one day. The tide was really strong, but we were young. We thought it was cool. We kept daring each other to go a bit further and a bit further. Before you know it, we were lost out at sea. I thought I was going to die. When I think back on what happened, I really wish I had. My board was spinning around and around. I was just trying to hang on to it when something pulled my leg. I didn't know what it was, but it was strong. It was gripping around my ankle and there was nothing I could do. I got one big tug. I plunged into the water and I kept my arms wrapped around my surfboard. Then there was another tug and I lost control altogether. It pulled me right down into the water and there was nothing I could do about it. It kept pulling. I kept going deeper and deeper and deeper. I had no chance to hold my breath. I could feel my lungs filling with water. I wondered how long I would have until I drowned."

"What was it? Pulling you?"

He turned and looked directly into my eyes. His torch lit up his face.

"It was a monster. A horrible beast with tentacles like a squid but the body of an old woman. Its face held nothing but evil. And I will kill it. I am here to destroy the monsters that live in the dark."

I remembered Mr Morris saying something about things that live in the dark.

"Anyway, that's not the important part. The important part is what happened next. After I got home."

"How did you escape?"

"I don't remember."

I laughed, and he shouted, "Boy, I am not lying to

you! This happened. As honest as I am stood here now. We woke up on the beach, my friends and me. We were tired and we were hungry. We couldn't stop sweating. We were all sick. I don't know how many times we threw up on that beach just trying to find our way back to the hotel. But what is truly terrifying is what happened to my friends. They... changed. Something happened to them down there in that water."

"My friends have come back changed too."

"Oh no they haven't. You misunderstand me. My friends *didn't* come back. And neither have yours. I believe that my friends are still down there under the oceans. That's if they still exist at all. It's more likely that they were fed to the beast in the water."

"But you said that they were on the beach with you. That you were all sick together."

"I thought that they were. But those things were not my friends. They were not boys. They were something else entirely. They were part of her..."

"Lowenna," I said. It was not a question. I knew exactly what he meant.

He nodded grimly. "That woman. She's the root of all of this. My so-called friends started to look more human by the day, but when they first arrived, there was something very wrong about them. They had gills on their necks and their fingers were joined up. They were fish-folk. Horrible things. My theory is that these disgusting creatures become for fishlike in the water but more human on land. She sent them to go back to our parents and spread into our community. Imagine it. Those things walking among us. In our shops. Walking down our streets. And you don't if they're us or not. They would have managed it if I hadn't stepped in."

"What did you do?"

"We had a boat that Lowenna liked to take us out on for sailing trips. I convinced the boys that we should celebrate our last day at the hotel by going out on our own. No fisherman. No grown-ups. Just us. They were happy to do it. Happy enough to just be around the water, I reckon. I took them out forty-five minutes out to sea. And then I killed them." He said it so calmly, as though he was telling me what time it was. "I gutted them the way you gut any fish. I threw their bodies into the sea. If nothing else, I hoped it would act as a warning to the rest of those beasts. When I got back, I expected the wrath of Lowenna. But nothing came. The boys' parents were contacted, and they were told that, tragically, their boys had drowned when we had gone surfing. They told them that I was the only survivor, and I was the only boy to go back to my parents after the accident."

"But you- You don't know that. You were only little. You were unwell. How do you know you weren't imagining it?"

He looked serious. "Oh, I know I wasn't imagining it. I've been doing this a long time you know. I watch them. They bring children here every single year. And it happens over and over. Every year, they go to the beach. Every year, they are pulled under. And every year, something that looks like them, *but isn't*, crawls out of the water and back."

"And you kill them?"

"I wish. I've been formulating my plan. I can't go around murdering children all the time, as much as I would like to. But I knew I needed to save *you*. I couldn't stand by and allow you to go under."

"Me? Why me? Why am I so special?

"Because you are my son."

CHAPTER 19

The Sleeping Lighthouse Children

"Yes, I'm your father. Goodness knows what my brother's playing at, sending you here."

"So is my mum here too?"

"You mum? No, I don't see her anymore. Truth be told, she never really believed me when I told her about this stuff"

"But I really am your son?"

"For the last time, yes. How many times do I have to tell you that?"

"So why don't I live with you?"

"Are you crazy? Did you think I'd let a kid of my own live around here? As soon as we knew your mum was pregnant, I insisted that we move away. Only... I couldn't do it. I'd spent far too long on my plan. I had to save the children who were coming here every year. So, we reached an impasse. I couldn't let your mother and you stay here but I couldn't leave myself. I just couldn't. This was my quest. You were my treasure."

"I can't believe it"

"That proves it then."

"What do you mean?"

"If you don't believe me, then that's proof that you are my son. Your mother never believed any of my *crazy stories* either. We argued about it a lot. And of course, now, she's gone. So that's how that went."

Even though I said that I didn't believe him, I couldn't help but look at the man who'd claimed to be my father. I'd always tried to picture my dad in my head. I wondered if he would look like me. And you know what? This man – my father or not – certainly did. He had the same curly brown hair. He had the same hooked nose.

"And now I hope you understand why I've been tracking you ever since I knew you were on this trip. I kept track of your age. It's always when the kids are twelve that they come here. I've been following you this whole time. But she's had her dogs on me. I've been hanging around outside the hotel, but how could I not? I had to make sure that you were okay. And when I heard about the boat ride- Well, I couldn't let that go ahead. No wonder I destroyed the boat the way I did. Anyway, as she goes back to the hotel, I'm sending you on you back home."

"What?"

"I'm sending you as far away as I can."

"I can't go. They've got my friends. I need to rescue them."

He stopped. He turned and smiled at me.

"You're definitely my son."

We came to a staircase cut into the stone. We climbed in silence for a long time. I was too busy thinking about what he had told me. I don't know what he was thinking about. Eventually we came a point when the stairs stopped. There was a solid ceiling above us. The man reached up and revealed that it was a trap door. He turned the handle and revealed the key lock. He pulled a small shiny key from one of his many pockets and opened the door.

We emerged into a completely circular room. The ceiling reached on high above us and there were windows in every direction.

"This is a lighthouse," I said.

"It certainly is. This is the only place where I can keep my eyes on everything that goes on around here. This is my base of operations."

Apart from the setting outside and the strange shape of the building, it just looked like a regular home. There was a kitchen with a sink and an oven. There was a couch. I could see a door that I assumed lead to his bedroom.

"Come upstairs," he said.

We continued up the winding staircase until we

came to another door. This time, he pulled out a key of his own and opened the door.

"Now, this is more like it," I couldn't help but shout. This was like a real spy's hideout. He had a wall covered in pieces of paper with different bits of information on them. There were maps and photos and lists. I saw photos of everyone in my class. There were Thomas and Ruby and Grace. But that was nothing compared to the pictures of me. There was my year 6 school photo. There were pictures of me getting onto the school bus and photos that were taken through the windows of the hotel. There was even one of me sleeping. Every piece of paper had a pin in it and there were strings connecting them, I assume showing some fact which joined up all these crazy occurrences together.

There was a solid, green door. It had a window, but the shutter was closed.

"What's in there?" I asked.

"I'm glad you asked. That's the most important thing in this room. He pulled back the shutter.

"Are those?"

"Yes. Those are your classmates. Or the ones I could reach, at least." I could see Grace. She was asleep. They were all asleep. I felt in my pocket and I looked at the Grace that was laying on the bed in the other room. That girl was not wearing her beaded bracelet. That meant that she must have been the real Grace! "Haven't got time to explain. Long story short, when those kids were thrown in there with the sea monster, I threw this on and went in after them." He held up a scuba suit.

"Well, that's great," I cried. They're saved, we can all go home like nothing ever happened."

"Oh, I wish that was true, Jack. The truth is that I may have made this whole thing worse just to rescue these kids. Why do you think they bring them here every single year? Exactly at the same date?" He walked over to the board with all the papers. "I've been piecing it together and I've determined two probable explanations for what's going on here. There is something big and deadly down there that is feeding on these children and is laying eggs to replace them. I don't know how she makes them look just like real people but because they end up looking human, it means that they can blend in with us like nothing ever happened and nobody questions it. It's what makes guys like me look crazy, because I'm one of the few who says what's going on. Now here are the two options. Either, A: this thing has to eat every twelve months. If this is the case, then I've deprived it of food and it's going to be very hungry. If that's true, then I don't know how it's going to react." A chill ran down my spine. "Or, B: It takes twelve months to lay its eggs. Clearly it uses its victims to model its children on. Without that model, I think we're going to see these things as they really are. Ugly and hungry and evil. And they're going to be coming for us, a whole army of teeth and tentacles."

We stood in silence for a moment. Finally, I said, "I don't know your name."

"Huh? I guess you don't, do you? It's Chris."

"Chris," I said, and I smiled. "Although I guess for me, I'd have to call you Dad"

I pushed the green door and went to see my friends. But before I could enter, Chris put his arm out to stop me.

"What are you doing?"

"Not so fast, Jack. You don't get to live as long as me by trusting everyone you meet. Come with me. I need to do another test on you."

CHAPTER 20
The Test

He slammed the door shut, slid the window cover over and bolted the door. We went back downstairs and, this time, used the front door. Chris nodded that I should walk through it, which I did. The storm had died down a little now, but the wind was still blowing strongly.

"Keep walking," he said.

What was he doing? The coast? After everything he'd been telling me about the dangers of the sea.

I stood in the sand, the water coming up occasionally and touching my trainers.

"Keep going. Until the water comes up to here." He held his hand up to his waist.

"You can't be serious."

"Do I look serious?" He pulled out a gun.

"What are you doing? Oh my god, Dad. What are you doing with a gun?"

"Until the water comes up to here," he repeated. This time, he held the gun up to his waist.

I kept walking.

"The water is getting into my trousers."

"You'll live," he said. I wasn't so confident that I would.

When the water reached my bellybutton, he shouted, "Okay, stop right there." He stood about two metres from me and pointed the gun at my face.

"How do I know that you're you? Why should I believe that you are really my son, Jack Williams?"

"Of course I'm me!"

"But you would say that, wouldn't you?"

"Well I'm not one of those fish things, but there's no way I can prove it one way or another, can I?"

"Of course, we can. We can have an old-fashioned witch trial."

"What do you mean?" But what he meant became immediately obvious. He rushed towards me, grabbed me by the collar and pushed my down into the water. The first thing I noticed was the taste of salt in my mouth. Then I felt the burn as the water rushed into my mouth and into my lungs. I pushed back, trying to stand, but I wasn't strong enough. He held me down with one hand, I could feel the steel of the gun against the back of my head. I thought I was going to drown.

He pulled me up. "Show me your neck!" I coughed

and a bubble of water came out of my mouth. I could feel him handling my neck. He pushed my ears forward to look behind them. He shoved me back under.

The salt. The burn. I was at least a little more ready for it this time. I took a breath and held my mouth shut. He held me for twice as long and shook me under the water, his fingers feeling around my neck. He pulled me up again. He held my hair and pointed the gun at me with his other hand. He came up really close and inspected my eyes and lips.

"Please," I said, feeling myself beginning to cry. "Please don't do this. I'm not one of them. I promise."

CHAPTER 21

<u>And When You Gaze Long Enough into an Abyss…</u>

"Dad, it's me! They didn't do anything to me. I wouldn't let them."

"I believe you. But I can't afford to just trust you."

We had been at this for a while. He would hold me in. He would check me over while I pleaded that I was innocent. Then he would thrust me back in and we would repeat. He pulled me up again and this time, finally, he stopped.

I tried to beg but I just coughed up a load of water. "Plea- gugh- pluh-"

"Shut up!" he shouted. "Shut up and let me look at you."

I rubbed water out of my eyes. When I could see again, I saw that he was frozen. His urgency was gone and replaced with a silent study.

"I don't believe it," he said.

"I'm human. I told you."

"You little liar. Look at you. You're one of them."

"Are you crazy?"

"Your lips are enormous. And your eyes. You're one of those things!"

He was shaking with anger.

"Look at me," I cried. You're being ridiculous. Look at me."

"I'm so disappointed. I really hoped that I'd be able to save Jack. I thought I could get to him in time." He remembered that he was holding the gun. He cocked it and pointed it at me. I felt tears well up in my eyes.

I fell down into the water, but I hadn't slipped. Something was gripping my leg. I fought against it and tried to swim but I couldn't move my legs. Either of them. Something strong and sticky was wrapped around my calves, clenching them close together and tugging at me. I heard a huge bang and realised that Chris must have fired the gun.

I didn't have time to absorb anything that was happening. I was plunging deep into the water. Something I did notice, however, was that all of a sudden, I was not finding it so difficult to breathe. If anything, I was suddenly finding that everything seemed really natural. My heart was slowing down to a regular beat. I was feeling less scared of the tentacle pulling me down. The fear of the madman with the gun up above wasn't bothering me anymore. I tried to blink and found that I couldn't. But the light adjusted, and everything became clearer.

I looked down and saw what was pulling on my leg. A purple tentacle, like the one I'd seen that morning at Merlin's cave was wound around my ankle four or five times. I could see circular puckers up and down one side of it. They were sticking to my ankle and throbbing as they sucked on my leg. The tentacle seemed to extend endlessly into the depths of the deep.

And then I saw it. The mouth beckoned and opened wide. I was rapidly approaching some faceless void. A million eyes of different sizes pointing in different directions turned to watch my arrival. Getting closer, I saw that the eyes all belonged to the same hideous void. Teeth slowly protruded until they were long spears pointing at all three hundred and sixty degrees of the open mouth with no hint of a lip to suggest the top or bottom. It was merely and purely a devouring abyss.

Still I was pulled faster and faster. My heart stopped, as I was overcome by my own smallness as the thing filled everything I could see. I saw that the tentacle that had hold of me began at the centre of the mouth, and I knew my fate. I saw the grime on the fangs, and spots of red from previous victims.

As I thought I was about to be devoured, a voice called out, in a language I had never encountered but somehow understood, "Stop!"

JOSHUA JAMES POTTS

And everything went black.

CHAPTER 22
<u>… the Abyss Also Gazes into You</u>

When I opened my eyes, I was somewhere very familiar and, at the same time, very strange. I walked, or rather swam, through what I recognised to be the entrance hall of my home. And yet, when I stopped to think about it, I realised I had never been here before. This place was completely alien to me, but I seemed to know every inch of it, like I'd lived here my whole life. I could see photos on the wall. Photos of my family. Photos that I recognised, without remembering ever posing for them. But something was missing from the photos. People were missing. In fact, the only person that was present in any of the photos was mum. And I knew it was my mum. How did I know that? I didn't know what she looked like. I'd never seen a picture of her. I had no memory of her. But it was definitely her. I *knew* it. She sat grinning in the restaurant where I celebrated my tenth birthday party. I remembered the photograph. I remember having a mouthful of chocolate birthday cake when my uncle shouted, "Say cheese!". But I wasn't in the photo. Mum was in the photo, but her eyes were huge and white, with no pupil to show where she was looking. Her grinning lips were bloated and puffy. And there they were. Rows of gills on her neck, just under her ears. I continued along the corridor. There was our holiday photo. Mum was sat in a rollercoaster on her own, with nobody sitting beside her or in the carriages behind her. The eeriest of all: my school photo. An empty frame showing nothing but a blueish purple background and a wooden stool with no little boy sat on top of it.

"This has got to be, hands down, the weirdest holiday I've ever been on in my entire life," I said to myself.

Creak.

It came from the top of the stairs. I knew it came from the top of the stairs because I knew the house and I knew that particular stair creaked.

"You're home," she gushed. "I knew you'd come home."

The bizarre fishlike woman I had seen in my family photographs glided down the staircase, not using the steps. Apart from all the changes, it was Mum. Right down to her clothes. She swept me up in a webbed-fingered embrace. She smacked bloated kisses on my cheek.

"My little boy is back! Just wait until your father hears about this."

"My dad is here?"

"Just on his way home from the office. He'll be so happy to have you here. Well, I guess I'm going to have to stretch dinner to an extra plate, aren't I? No, don't be sorry. You get yourself off to the bathroom and wash before dinner. You remember where everything is?"

I nodded. As weird as everything was, it was true. I did remember where everything was.

I found myself gliding effortlessly up the stairs. I turned left and opened the bathroom door. I locked it behind myself and tried to ground myself. I sat on the toilet and put my head in my hands. When I opened my eyes again, the true absurdity of my surroundings struck me. I was underwater. This bathroom was full of water. The toilet that I was sat on had water flowing lazily in and out of it. I had to laugh. It made the whole point of a bathroom pointless. As I laughed, bubbles popped out of my mouth. I turned the tap on, and nothing happened. How could it? There was water everywhere anyway.

But then I looked in the mirror at myself. It was me, and it wasn't. I had the same curly brown hair, but I didn't have big brown eyes that everyone knows me for. Instead, I had two huge egglike white domes in my face. I had no pupils. That answered my question about Grace. No, she couldn't see her own brain. She could see forwards just as normal. Just as I could right now. Because whatever had happened to her was happening to me now. I had become one of them. I didn't know how. I didn't know why, but it was the unavoidable truth.

I began to cry. Nobody would have known if they could have seen me because my tears floated away into the surrounding water. I was horrific. My face was swollen. My ears had fallen back into my head and everything else had protruded forwards. I held up my hands and saw that my fingers were joined together with flaps of thin, stretchy skin.

I swam down to the dining room as quickly as I could.

"What is happening to me?"

"Did you wash for dinner?"

"I said, what is happening to me?"

"Hush now, I've been waiting for you and your father for long enough. Don't go ruining this for me."

I stood stubbornly, trying to look angry with my new face.

She sighed. "Just sit down and we'll talk over dinner. Now, take these and set the table."

I put three placemats and three sets of cutlery on the table. I took glasses out of the cupboard and then, laughing at the ridiculousness of it, put them by the placemats without filling them. I couldn't see the point. Then I sat at my seat and waited as patiently as I could.

But she was the first to speak. "Nothing is happening to you, my dear."

"But- I mean *something* is obviously happening. Look at me!"

She chuckled and took two plates out of the cupboard and lined them up on the counter.

"You are reverting."

"Reverting? Reverting to what?"

"To your true self. You've been away from the water for so long. You look confused, sweetheart."

"Too right, I'm confused!"

"You were born in the water."

Well, that was true. Hadn't I been bragging about it to Ruby? Telling her that I was a water baby, and all that. How right I had been without realising it.

"Our people change when we are out of the water. You're returning to your natural ways."

"My natural ways?"

She put our plates on the table and sat down with me.

"So that's why I didn't drown?" I asked.

"That's right. Simply put, we turn more human when we are on the land. When we are free to swim down in the depths, we return to this." She gestured to her puffed out lips.

I grabbed at my face and squeezed. "I can't believe this is happening to me."

"Nothing is happening to you. This is who you always were. What happened to you is what happened up there."

"No," I said, shaking my head. "You need to go right back to the beginning."

She sighed, looking annoyed, and began to eat her food. When she had swallowed the first bite, she spoke. "It all begins with a boy who would be your father. He lived up there on the land."

"Yes! Dad told me about that. And how he and his friends were pulled under the water by some sort of sea-monster."

She bristled at the word but then carried on. "Good! So, you do know some of the story. Well, there's a bit more to than that, but essentially, yes. He was up there on the beach with his friends when we brought him down here to our world. There is a thing that happens to us when we are born. It happened to me. It happened to your father."

"And did it happen to me?"

"Well- technically no, but really it never *needed* to happen to you."

"What does that mean?!"

"Will you let me get to it. So, *normally*, what happens is this: We cannot live down here forever. And we must feed on the landwalkers. To counter these problems, a tradition has been handed down for centuries. Our ancestors began it and we carry it on to this day. We bring down the offspring from the land, who are around the same age as our own children. There is a *bonding* and we come to resemble these humans. This is why I look so similar to this Savannah Williams woman, from the dry place. When the change is underway, and we begin to lose our gills, we are sent up. The whole process relies on complete secrecy, because when the parents don't realise what's going on, they take us in as if we were their own children. They don't know any better. They assume we're sick. And they take us home and we live with them and we grow."

I felt sick. I felt every hair on my body stand on end which I always thought was impossible under water. I imagined all the cities of England with these things walking among them. Nobody knowing any different, sometimes the things themselves not even knowing the difference. And then these horrible creatures meeting humans and marrying them and breeding with them and having more little half children. *Ugh*. The thought sickened me. But it all made sense. I thought of seeing my friends asleep in my father's lighthouse while their pretenders walked around at the Moonlight Hotel.

"And the human children, "I asked. "Do they grow up to be little fish babies here?"

This time, she stopped being annoyed and started to chuckle a little bit.

"Oh, Jack."

"What? What did I say that was so funny?"

"You've lived among humans your whole life and you say something as ridiculous as that? You know that humans can't breathe underwater."

"So, what do you do with them?"

She chuckled again and then said, "Eat your food, Jack" gesturing to my plate with her fork.

I looked down and almost screamed again. On my plate, along with some salad, a few chips and a dollop of tomato ketchup, was a boy's arm. The fingers curled up as though it was trying to catch a cricket ball. I wanted to be sick.

"You are what you eat," she said, chuckling again. "Okay, it's an old joke but we always tell it at this time."

"I'm not eating this."

"Don't be ridiculous, Jack. You need to eat this to grow big and strong. It'll put scales on your chest. Your father did and look how big and strong he is now."

"Don't be stupid," I snapped. "Nobody has eaten my father. I've met him. He's alive and kicking and absolutely bonkers." Well, maybe not as crazy as I had thought, I had to admit.

"Ah," she said. "You're right. You have met your father. Your *real* father. Your real father who ate his human copy when he went through the changing process."

I paused to digest what she was telling me. I thought of the boys that he had murdered.

"But he escaped. The other boys-"

"Oh, yes!" She was cackling with laughter this time. "I'd forgotten all about that. Thank you for reminding me, Jack! I needed a good laugh."

"Reminding you of what?"

"Your dad really did get the wrong end of everything, didn't he? Yes, those boys he'd been playing with had changed that day. But, so had he! He had somehow gotten it into his head that he was still human. He really was stubborn and couldn't accept the change. Yes, I know all about his little dark boat trip where he attempted to drown those two boys. Fancy that! He tried to drown a couple of fish!" She banged her fist on the table and threw her head back. She laughed with a wide-open mouth and food sprayed around the room. A bit of fingernail hit me on the cheek.

"So, they didn't die?"

"Of course they didn't die. They wriggled about a bit and then floated down here with the rest of us.

We waited a little bit and sent them back up again. It's sad when you think about it. I mean, they had to make it on their own, and those poor human parents who thought their sons had died. Well, I suppose they had died, but you know what I mean."

"So, dad spent his whole life thinking he was like m-thinking that he was human. And I- "

"You're special. You're a *native.* You were made when he was in human form. Your father didn't understand. I couldn't live like that. I passed you along to Chris's brother for safekeeping, and that, as they say, was that."

"No wonder they were so determined that I come here."

"Oh yes, you're a big deal, Jack. Everyone has been talking about you. Everyone's put a lot of effort in to get you down here. And now," she grinned, "you can stay here with me, forever."

"I can't stay here."

"Don't be silly. Now eat your arm."

"I'm not eating this."

"Jack, you're starting to annoy me. I've been waiting a long time for you to come back. And now you're misbehaving, asking too many questions and being rude about my cooking."

"It's not the cooking, it's- What am I saying? I need to go rescue my friends." I stood up urgently and made for the door.

"Jack, wait. You can't go back for those things. That's not what we are. That's not what we're about. I'm your family."

"No, you're not," I shouted. "You are not my family."

"You are my flesh and blood!"

"That's not what matters! I'm going back to the people who raised me and looked after me."

She threw down her cutlery and stood up.

"Why, you ungrateful little landwalker." She stood very slowly. Then she reached up to the holes in her face. She didn't have a nose. Not a real one. She had two little slots that bubbled occasionally. She stuck her fingers deep into them now. She pulled at her face and tore the skin off the front of her head. She grimaced and her thick lips pulled back. Her skin seemed to fall loose. It reminded me of a snake I'd seen at the zoo once. The zookeeper had explained to me that when a snake grows too big, it throws off its old skin and grows a new one that fits.

Out of the enormous hole that she had torn into her face, a monster emerged. Thousands of slithering tentacles writhed out of the hole and squirmed in every direction. Billions of little eyes sat atop these tentacles peering around every direction. She grew to an enormous size that seemed impossible to fit inside her human form.

It roared and hurled itself towards me.

CHAPTER 23
The Rescue

"You can't leave," my fish-mother screamed. You must stay here with me! You're one of us."

I didn't think. I simply swam. I kicked my feet and my hands and moved as quickly as I could. Before I knew it, I was out of the house and was travelling upwards and upwards. I was panting and couldn't catch my breath. I had a stitch in my side. I kept going. *She must be gaining on me,* I thought. *I just have to keep moving.*

But the strange thing is that she didn't seem to be following me. When I turned around to look, I found that there was nobody there. Where could she be? Why wasn't she chasing me?

I struggled to breathe when I reached dry land. I was back at Merlin's Cave. It kept coming back to here. I fell onto all-fours on the beach and coughed up gulps of water. I found the reverse was happening and now that I was in the air, it was hard to breathe. Not impossible, but it was difficult. That and the rapid chase I'd just been part of. I looked behind me like I was paranoid and looked at the sea. The water was still. Not even a ripple.

I ran into the cave and up the stairs. I took the steps two at a time until I came to the trap door. I turned the handle and climbed into the lighthouse. Determined to leave as quickly as possible, I went to the green door and pulled back the window cover. I saw my friends. I saw Ruby, Grace and Thomas, but this time, they were sitting up awake. I banged on the window. Ruby saw me and ran over. She staggered and stumbled but made it to the door. I must have looked horrifying because as soon as she reached the window she gasped.

"Jack!" she cried. "What on Earth happened to you?"

"There really isn't time to explain." I said. "Can you all run? We need to get out of here. Like, now."

Ruby nodded. A few of the others didn't look so sure. Grace was barely awake, but Thomas said, "Don't worry about her. I'll carry her."

"Then, let's go," I said. "Follow me."

I led them downstairs to where I knew the front door was. I kept looking around. Now that I was back, I remembered Chris, my unknowing fish-father. I had been so frightened of being eaten by a sea monster that I forgot that it's perfectly possible to die of everyday things, like your dad shooting you in the face as part of his monster killing crusade.

But he wasn't there. So far, so good. I took them through the front door, and as soon as I did, I could see why Chris chose this site as his base of operations. The lighthouse was on top of the tallest hill around and I could see everything. I could see the row of cliffs on the side with the winds crashing down on them. I could see the fields in the middle, and the ancient buildings further to right, connected by winding roads.

"Oh my God," said Ruby. "Look!"

The Moonlight Hotel had just about been hanging on a few days ago when we had arrived. But it wasn't going to be there for much longer. The monster that had emerged from the dead shell of my mother had grown to a colossal size. She was now twice the size of the Moonlight Hotel and was towering over it. She flailed out her tentacles and let out a hideous cry that sounded nothing like a human voice. The tentacles spread over the top the hotel and began to drag it into the ocean. On the first pull, tiles came off and the chimney slid down onto the ground below. At the second tug, the cliff itself began to give way and the half of the hotel that was closest to the sea plunged into it.

"I say it's an improvement," said Thomas, but he looked frightened. Everyone looked frightened. I looked- well, I probably looked more *frightening* than *frightened*, but I felt frightened.

"Where do we go now?"

"Look!" someone shouted. "The car! Do you see it?"

And there it was. My dad was speeding from the hotel to the lighthouse. *Coward*, I thought. *I thought you wanted to destroy that thing and now you're running away? I guess you're only brave enough to kill children.* The car stopped, he rolled the window down and fired a red flare high up into the sky. The monster turned and saw this with its billions of eyes. It tossed the remainder of the hotel into the ocean like it was just an annoyance and made its way towards the car. The car then resumed its journey.

"Brilliant," Thomas said. "He's luring it away"

"He's luring it straight to us!" shouted Ruby.

And she was right. The car was taking the road that lead directly up to this lighthouse.

CHAPTER 24

<u>The Man with the Magic Harpoon</u>

"Right kids. Get inside, all of you," Dad said as he pulled up.

He grabbed me around the scruff of the neck. "You don't leave my sight. I know a turncoat when I see one."

"I need to explain."

"No time." he marched inside and pulled the big handle on the wall. Several things happened at once. Bolts slammed down over all the doors and windows. The lighthouse plunged momentarily into darkness, and then the artificial lighting came on full blast, removing every shadow from the entire room. He powerwalked over to the cabinet, used two keys to open two different locks and swung the door open. Inside was something out of one of my war novels. There was a whole rack of sea-weapons. There were harpoons of all different sizes, with enormous blades that had jagged spikes down the side. The spears each had a small circular hole in the handle.

"That's awesome!" shouted Thomas.

"Come here," Chris said to Grace, who was still woozy. He put a harpoon into a harness by one of the windows. "I want you to stand here with this. Pull here to shoot. If that things get any closer, I want you to fire at it."

"Cool!" said Thomas. "What do you want us to do?"

"I don't want you to worry about the big'un. You're gonna stop the little guys."

"What little guys?"

"Oh my god," said Grace, from the window. "There are so many of them."

We fought to squeeze a look out of the tiny firing gap in the wall. What I saw nearly made me freeze. They were coming. The fish kids. But not just my class. Sure, they were there and I recognised many of them. But it seemed like every generation, year after year, of kids who'd been brought to the Moonlight Hotel as sacrifices were heading up to the lighthouse once. It was like an army of monsters. Those hideous faces, I thought, forgetting that I looked exactly like them now.

Chris was handing out pistols to a group of boys. Thomas was first in queue, eager for his gun, but he also handed one to Terry and one to Jerry. Terry looked as eager as Thomas, but Jerry looked nervous. Or maybe it was Terry.

"Each of you take a station, North, South and West." It was only then that I saw the true scope of what was coming for us. The whole army of kids, walking slowly like zombies out of the ocean. The ones at the front were waist deep in the water, walking as easily as if they were on the street. I could see kids further back, the tops of their heads poking out of the water, getting closer and closer so slowly, revealing more and more of their hideous figures. "If those things get to the lighthouse, they'll drag every last one of us into the ocean. I want you to make sure that doesn't happen." He slammed down an excessive amount of ammunition on the table next to each of the boys. He handed a walky-talky to Ruby. "Girl, come with me. This is the best spot to look out. If anything goes bad, I want you to ring me. I don't want to take this thing nuclear but if that's where things are, that's what I gotta do. If we're breached, I want you to use this." He opened a black case, which revealed three shiny grenades."

"Are you crazy?" I shouted.

"Shut your bloated mouth. You better believe I'm crazy. There are things in this building too precious to the survival of the human race. If you think they're going to get in, then we're going to blow this place to smithereens."

He is crazy!

They were getting closer now. Thomas let off a shot. I saw that he had holstered his handgun and instead had taken a sniper out of the cabinet of his own decision and was picking off kids his own age.

"That's good shooting kid," Chris said and cocked a shotgun one-handed. I'd only ever seen that done in movies, and despite everything going on around me, I couldn't help finding cool.

"Come with me," he said, and pulled me up the stairs. We ran up the winding staircase. Round and round, through doors, through trapdoors and all the way up until we reached the very top. Chris popped the trapdoor above our heads, and we found ourselves in the open air amidst the rain and the wind. There was a fog descending on the ground, I noticed. I worried that this would make things too difficult for my friends downstairs.

Chris set off more flares just like he had before. The monster's attention had been caught this time. It turned to look at us, but it didn't come closer. It seemed happy to let its children do all the fighting first.

I never liked chess. It's too hard. I joined the chess club once at school because I knew that Ruby was a member. I only lasted one lesson, but I remember someone telling me that you should keep your queen safe while you sacrifice all your less valuable pieces. Was that what the monster was doing now?

"Okay, we need to get her attention. Pass me that case. Carefully."

I saw a long black case with locks along the side. I grabbed the handle and it was really heavy. I picked it up with two hands and heaved it over to Chris. He unlocked it and threw it open as though he'd done this a million times.

"A bazooka!" I couldn't help crying out.

He smirked. "Watch this, kid"

He let one off and I watched it go directly into one of the monster's huge eyes. It exploded a with a huge bang and a spray of red light. That definitely got its attention. It let out an inhuman roar and its tentacles rushed to the eye as though it was rubbing the source of the pain. Then it pointed its body directly at us and started to run. *Run*, it was more like a gallop.

"That thing's so fast!" I said.

"Yeah, well so am I!" He reloaded and fired before I realised what he was doing. "Prepared for this day my whole life."

He looked around and frowned. "Okay, kid. I'm going to let you out of my eyes for one second, but you better come back. If I die because of you, you better believe I'm going to haunt you."

"What do you want?"

"Go get me one of the harpoon spears."

I didn't ask. I did as I was told. When I came back, he didn't seem so sure. He actually looked like he was panicking. "What are you looking for?"

"This little box. It's about this big and made of wood. Damn it. I think I left it at the boat."

"No, you didn't," I called, reaching into my jacket. I pulled the box out of my coat pocket and he opened it. There was a blue amulet on a golden chain. He snapped the chain and placed amulet in the gap of the spear. Suddenly, the whole spear began to glow. The light was blue. It seemed to throb, and the light grew brighter and darker over and over.

"You hold this. I'm gonna keep firing at it. When I say, I want you to hand me the spear."

"What are you going to do?"

"I'm going to end this once and for all."

I could hear screams from down below. I couldn't believe that they still had any ammunition. They were firing so much.

"This is for my friends," he shouted and fired off another shot.

"Dad, I've got to tell you something."

"Now really isn't the time."

"Now is the only time. I need to tell you something about yourself."

"Not now!"

"Why haven't you killed me?"

"What?"

"Why haven't you killed me? You've dedicated yourself to destroying every last one of them. Why didn't you kill me the moment you knew what I was?"

"I'm a little busy here!"

"You know the truth, don't you? You know that you're one of them. We both are. That's why I'm like this. You didn't survive that day you went into the water. You were just like those other boys. Monsters, all of us."

"That's not true!"

"You know it is! It doesn't make any sense the other way. Why didn't one of those things ever turn up looking like you?"

He turned to look at me, but his face wasn't angry. He looked sad. He looked scared. But not scared of dying. He looked scared that hearing me say these words and believing them would finally make them true.

"I have to end this," he said, firing off another round. The creature's eye burst in a wet "pop" and a gush of purple gunge exploded out of it. The creature didn't rub its pained eye this time. This time, it screamed and throw itself with all its force, every tentacle reaching for us. It was metres away now. It opened its mouth wider than I'd seen before. An enormous black abyss approached me, larger than the lighthouse itself. Teeth lined the entire mouth showing no up nor down, merely a thing meant to hurt and tear and kill and digest.

Chris put his hand on my shoulder and said, "I'm sorry. But this has to be done. This is revenge for making us this way."

Before I could say anything, he shouted, "Now!" He took the glowing spear and ran. He ran to the edge of the roof and leapt with the spear pointed out, glowing powerfully. I felt so proud in that moment. My dad looked like one of the illustrations in my fantasy novels. Like a warrior ready to slay a dragon, a beast much older and powerful than himself. His scream was louder than the wind or the monster. The mouth closed around them and he was gone.

There was a moment where nothing happened and then, suddenly, the beast glowed blue just like the spear had. Its tentacles were grabbing all over itself, trying to make sense of the pain. And I knew it *was* pain. Even in this entirely alien form, I could see the agony that it was feeling. The eyes rolled around in its head and it began to fall. It rolled down the side of the lighthouse and plunged into the depths of the ocean below.

I looked over the edge and shouted "Dad!" but I knew it was pointless. He was gone, swallowed up by the sea. *There are things more evil and powerful than you know that dwell in the dark places.*

I threw open the trap door and ran downstairs.

"Hey Jack!" Ruby shouted. "That thing. Is it dead?"

"No idea. What about those kids?"

Thomas had stopped firing. "They're not coming for us anymore."

"Look!" said Ruby and she pulled me over to the window gap. They had turned, each and every one of them and they were marching back towards the sea. I considered how strange it was that those things were compelled to do the same thing together. *Those things?* Was I not one of them? Did I have a compulsion to walk back into the sea? Actually, I did. But mine was to find my father. To find out if he had survived. And to make sure that the monster was truly dead.

"Let's go!" I shouted. "Come on! They're not coming for us anymore. We're going to take the car."

"Where are we going to go?" Grace asked.

We looked at each other and, when nobody answered, we walked solemnly to the car. All eight of us squeezed into Chris's four-seater.

"Umm, does anyone know how to drive?"

"My dad used to take me quad biking before he died," said Thomas.

"Uh, anyone else?" asked Ruby. "Only joking. Thomas, you take the wheel."

I believe that Thomas had used to be a really good quad biker when his dad was alive, but I also guess that it was probably a long time ago. He was really rusty, and although he didn't like to admit it, he couldn't really reach the pedals properly. The car jerked a lot, and the engine roared really loudly when we set off.

"You need to put it into second gear," said Ruby."

"Alright, alright, they don't have these on the quads."

We made it into town in once piece, which was remarkable considering everything that happened. We found Mr Morris sat outside of a pub. He was very impressed that Mrs Moon "had brought in driving lessons in lieu of the boat ride," although he did consider us a little bit too young for that sort of thing.

He was horrified when he saw the rubble that had once been the Moonlight Hotel, although his reaction was not what we had expected. I thought that he was going to go nuts, but we tried a different tactic. We simply owned up to it.

"It was our fault, sir. I guess we weren't doing what we were told, and we ended up knocking the hotel off the cliff."

"Well, I'm not pleased. I'm very disappointed. Horrified, in fact. But I'm glad that you told me the truth."

DAY FOUR

Epilogue

None of us had never been so ready to leave a place. We stayed at the Morrigan Inn, which was further into the town and seemed far enough from the craziness of the sea. That night, we all snuck into Grace's room because we didn't want to be alone, but Mr Morris turned up to send us all back to our individual rooms.

I got up in the middle of the night to go to the toilet. I spent a long time staring at myself in the mirror. It looked like my gills had finally disappeared. My lips and eyes had started to go back to normal, but not completely.

Our families came to pick us up the next day. "I hope they weren't too much trouble, Mr Morris," Paul was saying. He was wearing a polo shirt with the collar popped up and he had his sweater on his back tied around his neck.

"Well, I'd love to tell you that they weren't. But they were certainly a bit of a handful. Kept wandering off, both of them." Paul gave us both a dirty look.

"Yep, I had to round them up on not just one occasion."

"I bet they were bickering too, were they?" asked Sarah.

"Well, I can't say that for certain, but I'll tell you what I can tell you. You see that hill there.

Well that's where we were staying. That's where the Moonlight Hotel was. And now, thanks to your kids, it's at the bottom of the ocean." Sarah laughed touched Mr Morris on the arm for a few seconds. I think she thought Mr Morris was joking. Mr Morris said, "Yes, well. I have the rest of the kids to see off. So... Thank you for coming, and uh. Have a safe trip."

Before we got in, we said goodbye to the other kids. I saw Grace and Thomas go around the side of the hotel. I think they were kissing. Ruby obviously thought the same thing because she approached me sheepishly. "So, I guess I'll see you on Monday, Jack. I just wanted- you know, I just thought I'd better say thank you for saving me. Us. I mean, but thanks for everything. You were incredible."

"Well, it wasn't just me. We all pitched in. I couldn't have done it without you."

She giggled and leaned forward. She pushed her lips out and leaned in for a kiss. I took a big step back.

"I'll see you on Monday, Ruby. Thanks for everything."

I threw my bag in the boot of the car and climbed into the back seat. I felt bad for Ruby, but I couldn't get the image of that fish face puckering up for a kiss out of my head. I heard the boot slam and Grace climbed in next to me. My auntie and uncle said goodbye to everyone, and they got in the front seats.

"Have you buckled up?" said Paul.

"Yes," Grace said. I put my seatbelt on, and we set off.

"Well, I can't believe you two."

"I can," said Sarah. This is just like you two. We can't take you anywhere. I hope you know that we cut our trip short because of this."

"Sorry," we both groaned together. We had no energy to argue. We were just too relieved to be safe again.

"And you're having no more of your zombie books, Jack. They obviously have a negative effect on your character. You can read books like that when you're more mature. When you're fifteen or sixteen, and you start acting a responsible adult."

"And I think that Thomas is a negative influence on you, Grace. I don't think I want you hanging around that boy anymore. And don't think we didn't notice that girl who was sniffing around you too, Jack."

"Yes well, he can't help that," said Sarah. "He is such a handsome little man. But still, just you keep your eyes on your books. But not these books."

After about an hour or so, they tired themselves out and the journey went from annoying to just boring. We stopped at a service station, but it was a different one to the one we'd stopped at on the way to Tintagel. We all went to the toilet and jumped back in the car. My auntie and uncle swapped over, and

Sarah drove us from then on. Paul put his collar down and went down for a nap, resting his head by turning his seatbelt into a little hammock.

Grace gasped. I started to ask her what was wrong, but she put her finger to her lips. She tapped her phone. She began typing furiously on her phone and a second later my own mobile phone vibrated in my pocket. I pulled it out and opened the text:

> Dad's neck

Huh? I looked at Paul's neck, and saw it immediately. In the gap, where he had rolled his collar down, there were five rows of parallel gills.

THANK YOU FOR READING!

Before you go, I would like to give you a huge, sincere thank you for reading "The Monster at the Moonlight Hotel." It was an absolute joy to write, and I hope that you enjoyed Jack Williams' terrifying adventure.

If you had fun reading this book, please leave a review at Amazon. I am a self-published author, and the recommendation from readers like you goes a very long way in getting the word out there. If you could take a minute to tell people why you enjoyed it, that would be wonderful. If not, please select how many stars you think this story is worth.

Thank you again for joining me on this adventure. See you in the next one!

BOOKS BY THIS AUTHOR

Terry The Terrible Elf

Two heart-warming stories about the world's worst Christmas elf! In his debut book, Joshua Potts brings us Terry, the elf who wants everything to be perfect, but who keeps getting things wrong!

Also including, Terry the Terrible Elf: Lockdown!

It is a difficult time for everyone and the world is locked down due to the pandemic crisis. When Terry the Terrible Elf is sent home from the workshop due to an outbreak of "Sniffling sickness", he develops a plan to bring Christmas to families, even when they have to social distance. Once again, Joshua Potts proves that love and magic can be found even when things look hard!

ABOUT THE AUTHOR

Joshua Potts

Joshua Potts is a writer, actor and teacher based in Manchester, UK.

As a child, Joshua was a voracious reader of any book he could get his hand on but his favourites were always those with strange worlds and quirky characters. He started writing his own stories at a very young age and as an adult, he remains attracted to off-the-wall ideas. He lists his main influences as Edgar Allan Poe, Robert E. Howard and Stan Lee, among many, many others.

Joshua achieved his Masters Degree in Theatre: Writing, Directing and Performance at the University of York, where he wrote a play for his dissertation.

In his spare time, Joshua looks out of the window and waits for the lockdown to end.

Facebook: Joshua Potts, Author
Twitter: AuthorPotts
YouTube: Joshua Potts

Printed in Great Britain
by Amazon